Chicago Underground 2015

Rough

Skye Warren

Thank you for reading the Chicago Underground series! You can join my Facebook group for fans to discuss the series here: Skye Warren's Dark Room. And you can sign up for my newsletter to find out about new releases at skyewarren.com/newsletter.

Enjoy the story…

PROLOGUE

I HUGGED MY knees and stared at the strip of plastic on my bed. A small part of my brain knew it was weird to have it on the comforter, something I'd peed on. The rest of me was too busy freaking out to care.

One night I'd rather forget. The word *no* said and ignored. A little plus sign in an oval window. The dominoes fell, one after the other, leading to this...

Pregnant.

"Maybe it's wrong," Shelly whispered, her eyes wide. It took a lot to shock my best friend, but this had done it. Her face was pale, body as tense and still as mine.

I shook my head. "I've missed my period twice now."

Her blue eyes questioned me. "I thought you two weren't..."

Of course she guessed who the father was. Andrew. He'd been my other best friend. And definitely the only boy I would have trusted with my virginity. Only, I hadn't trusted him. Or just hadn't liked him that way. And trust? That had turned out to be a mistake.

That was a lesson I'd never forget. Trust was an awful mistake.

"We weren't," I said, my voice hoarse. We weren't

together, weren't dating. Weren't having sex, if you didn't count that one awful night.

"Then how?" she asked with a slow blink, uncomprehending. She didn't *want* to comprehend, and God, I wished I didn't have to live with the knowledge either. I wished it were a physical thing I could cut out of my skin. But it was just a memory—and memories lived forever.

I said nothing else as I stared at the plastic strip. As a tear fell down my cheek.

Said nothing, even when Shelly sucked in a breath.

She'd lived through her own daily hell. Maybe that was why she figured it out, when another teenaged girl might have taken my tears for regret. Or maybe she noticed too, how angry he'd become in the weeks and months before.

She hesitated. "Did he… did he force you?"

"No," I lied, my voice hollow. "Of course not."

Even on that night I knew I'd never tell anyone what had happened. Not Shelly. And definitely not the police. If they couldn't protect Shelly from her own father, how could they protect me? They wouldn't believe me. I'd take the words—the confession, the shame—and bury them deep. So deep no one could ever hear them. Not even me.

Shelly heard them, though. Her expression turned cold. "I'll kill him."

My heart clenched. I hated him for what he did. But I loved him as my friend, the one who'd hung out every afternoon and made me smile when my dad hadn't been back in months. Most of all, I understood him—more than I wanted to. I knew what went on at his house, even if he'd never actually told me. We were all broken, and we turned on each other with our fear and our fists. It was a cold way to live. A familiar one.

My hands curled into fists, grief and anger and anguish all at once. "He's gone."

Shelly shut her eyes, pain clear on her face. We both knew he'd skipped town suddenly.

I just hadn't told her why.

I'd never wanted her to know. Never wanted anyone to know about the choking terror of that night. And now there was a permanent reminder, a living memory of the worst moments of my life. A baby. I forced myself to think the words. There was a baby inside me right now.

What was I going to do with a baby?

Drop out of school. Get a job. Buy diapers. A sob escaped me, dry and hard.

The bedroom door opened. It took both of us a second to register. No one else was here. No one else was *ever* here. For one brief second, I thought it was *him*. Maybe Andrew had come back. Maybe, despite the awfulness of what he'd done, he'd find a way to help.

And God, I needed help from somewhere.

It wasn't Andrew. It was my father, back early from a long haul to California.

"You girls want some pizza?" His gaze narrowed on the white strip on the bed. "What the hell is that?"

I grabbed the pregnancy test and shoved it behind me. "Nothing."

My father stepped forward, his weathered face dark, eyes filling with rage. "That better belong to your friend there. She looks the type to get knocked up."

My jaw clenched. "Don't talk about her like that."

"Then it's yours?" He stepped forward. In the small room, that brought him right next to me. In a flash he'd twisted my arm. With a cry, I dropped the test to the ground. "Is that what you been doing in this room every time I'm on the road? Fucking around?"

"No," I cried, and it didn't matter that it was the truth. I'd never fucked around, not on purpose. Even that one time, when I hadn't wanted it, it hadn't been here. The truth didn't matter, though. Trust didn't matter.

He picked up the pregnancy test and stared at it.

I begged him, but only in my mind. *Try to understand. Support me. Please.*

I need you to be my dad now.

"Get out," he said, his voice low. "You want to spread your legs and get yourself knocked up? Get the fuck out of my house."

I stood there, frozen. Even when he picked up my lamp and threw it to the wall.

It shattered and fell to the carpet in a thousand pieces.

Shelly grabbed my hand and pulled me out of the room—and out the front door. The white strip of plastic came flying out the door after us. It landed in the dirt at my feet. I looked up at the house, knowing it would be the last time I was ever here.

Maybe the old manufactured double-wide wasn't much by some standards, but it was my home. And maybe my dad was gone more than he was here. But this had been my life. I hadn't wanted it to end. Hadn't been ready for it to be over. How was I going to live now?

I pressed a hand to my stomach. How was I going to support this baby?

I didn't know the answers. The only thing I knew was that I'd figure it out alone. Or with Shelly. But I would never again trust a man. I'd never give him the chance to hurt me or throw me out.

Never again.

CHAPTER ONE

THERE'S A CERTAIN sultry walk a woman has when she's bare that can't be faked. No hose and no panties. The nakedness under my skirt was as much about keeping me aroused as it was about easy access.

I'd perfected the art of fuck-me clothes. A surprising number of men asked me out, even at a grungy club on a Saturday night. Cute little college girl, they thought, out for a good time. I saved us all time by dressing my part.

Tonight's ensemble consisted of a tight halter and short skirt with cheap, high-heeled sandals, bouncing hair, and bloodred toenails. The scornful looks of the other women didn't escape me, but I wasn't so different from them. I wanted to be desired, held, touched. The groping fingers might be a cheap imitation of intimacy, its patina cracked with rust and likely to turn my skin green, but they were all I deserved.

My gaze panned to the man at the bar, the one I'd been watching all night. He nursed a beer, his profile harsh against the fluid backdrop of writhing bodies. His gray T-shirt hung loose on his abs but snug around thick arms, covering part of his tattoo.

Dark eyes tracked me the way mine tracked him.

His expression was unreadable, but I knew what he wanted. What else was there?

He was hot in a scary way, and that was perfect. Not that I was discerning. I needed sex, not a life partner. There were plenty of men here, men whose blackened pasts matched my own, who'd give it to me hard.

A woman approached him. Something dark and decidedly feminine roiled up inside me.

She was gorgeous. If he wanted to score, he probably couldn't do better, even with me.

I tried not to stare. She walked away a minute later—rejected. I felt unaccountably smug. Which was stupid, since I didn't have him either. Maybe no one had a chance with this guy. I was pretty enough, in a girl-next-door kind of way. Common, though, underneath my slutty trappings—brown hair and brown eyes were standard issue around here.

"Hey, beautiful."

I glanced up to see a cute guy wearing a sharp dress shirt checking me out. Probably an investment banker or something upstanding like that. Grinning and hopeful. Had I ever been that young? No, I was probably younger. At nineteen I had seen it all. The world had already crumbled around me and been rebuilt, brick by brick.

"Sorry, man," I said. "Keep moving."

"Aww, not even one dance?"

His puppy-dog eyes cajoled a smile from me. How nice it might feel to be one of the girls with nothing to worry about except whether this guy would call tomorrow morning. But I was too broken for his easy smile. I'd only end up hurting him.

"I *am* sorry," I said, wistfulness seeping into my voice. "You'll thank me later."

Regret panged in my chest as the crowd sucked him back in, but I'd done the right thing. Even if he were only interested in a one-night hookup, my type of sex was too toxic for the likes of him.

I turned back to the guy at the bar. He caught my eye, looking—if possible—surlier. Cold and mean. Perfect. I wouldn't taint him, and he could give me what I craved. Since Tall, Dark, and Stoic hadn't deigned to make a move on me, I would do the pursuing. A surprising little twist for the night, but I could go with it.

I squeezed in beside him at the bar. Up close his size was impressive and a little intimidating, but that only strengthened my resolve. He could give me what I needed.

"Hey, tough guy," I shouted over the din.

He looked up at me from his beer. I faltered a bit at the total lack of emotion in his face and fought an automatic instinct to retreat. His eyes were a deep brown, almost pretty, but remote and flat. Dark hair was cut short, bristly. His nose was prominent and slightly crooked, like it had been broken. Maybe more than once.

He looked mean, which was a good thing, but I was used to a little more effort. Even assholes provided a fake smile or smarmy line for the sake of the pickup. There was a script to these things, but he wasn't playing his part.

My club persona and beer from earlier lent me confidence. Whatever was bothering him—a bad day at the construction site or maybe a fight with the old lady—I didn't care. He was here, so he needed this as much as I did.

I planted my elbow on the bar. "I saw you looking at me earlier."

He raised an eyebrow. I shrugged. He was making me work for it, but I found myself more amused than annoyed.

"Buy me a drink?" I asked.

He considered me, then nodded and signaled the bartender.

The beat of the club reverberated as I took a sip. "So do you talk?"

His lips twitched. "Yeah, I talk."

"Okay." I leaned in close to hear him better. "What do you talk about?"

He ignored my question—or maybe answered it—by asking, "What are you doing here?" Almost like he was asking something deeper, but that had to be the alcohol talking.

"I'm trying to get laid, that's what I'm doing here." I pulled off a breathy laugh I was pretty proud of.

He didn't react, didn't appear surprised or even interested, the bastard. He just looked at me. "Why?"

I decided on honesty. "Because I need it."

He seemed to weigh the truth of my words, then nodded toward the exit. "All right, let's go." He got up and threw some cash on the bar.

His easy acceptance caught me off guard, just for a moment. But it shouldn't have surprised me, because…well, because men always wanted sex. That's what I liked about them—they didn't even bother trying to hide it. It was worse when I hadn't seen it coming, when it had sneaked up on me—Now wasn't the time to think of that. It was never the right time to think of that.

He tucked his hand under my elbow, guiding me. He used his body to maneuver us through the crowd, almost as a shield. The whole thing was so gentlemanly, given what we were about to do, that I wondered if he'd heard me right. Maybe he'd want to get coffee or something, and wouldn't that be awkward all around?

But he was a man, and I was a woman wearing fuck-me clothes—this could only end one way.

When we exited the club, I couldn't help sucking in several deep breaths. Even the faint smell of street sewage was refreshing, washing the stench of smoke, alcohol, and countless perfumes from my lungs. I never liked the crowds. The press of bodies, the mingling smell of sweat, the small bumps from all around. Tiny violations that were somehow okay since everyone did it.

As my heart rate settled, he inspected me as if he could read me. He couldn't. "What's your name?" I asked to distract him.

"Colin. Yours?"

"Allie."

"Nice to meet you, Allie. Your place or mine?"

I was comfortable again. I knew this play: horny girl who can't wait to get naked.

"We don't need to go anywhere. Let's get started right here." I let a soft moan escape me and clasped myself to the brick wall named Colin. Never mind that I was dry as a bone. He wouldn't notice. They never did.

He raised his eyebrows. "In the parking lot?"

"Or in my car. Whatever. I just want you to do me."

"I'm not fucking you in a car. It's forty degrees out."

I was hardly in this for comfort. I'd done it in colder weather just this past winter. "I don't mind."

"Well, I do."

"Fine." I was willing to give him so much. Why couldn't he take it the way I wanted? "Then we can go to the motel over there. You're paying."

He didn't look happy. I wasn't either, but I couldn't budge on this. Going to an apartment might be the norm for hookups, but my hookups weren't normal.

Going to their houses where they might do God knows what was out of the question. And I wasn't about to bring one of these guys home.

"Not there," he said. "I'll pick the place."

CHAPTER TWO

I FOLLOWED HIS truck in my car to a motel about ten minutes away. When I pulled in, he waved me to a parking spot next to his truck and went into the office.

The place wasn't fancy, but the manicured shrubbery and freshly painted building proclaimed this was an entirely different kind of establishment than the dump by the club. No renting rooms by the hour here.

The sign out front advertised $119.99 a night. A typical price for Chicago, but I sweated the cost. The extravagance of my six-dollar drink from earlier paled in comparison.

What if it was too much money? I might not be worth it.

I kept watch on the frosted office door like he might disappear. Eight minutes later, he came out. My stomach clenched. He flashed a key and nodded toward the back before getting into his truck. I followed him in my car and pulled up beside him again.

It was dark back here. Deserted. The only light came from flickering, yellow lamps dimmed by tiny hordes of bugs. Scattered buildings slumbered around us like a nest of dragons, their snore the low drone from the appliances. It wasn't exactly safe. Technically that was what I wanted, but the allure of danger only worked up to a point.

He didn't come to my car. Instead he opened the motel room door and waited.

I could drive away. He probably wouldn't even come after me. Even if he could, if I drove somewhere safe—assuming there was such a place—there'd be nothing he could do.

But his solemn patience gave me the courage to open the car door and join him.

The stale air and harsh edge of cleaning supplies softened me. I'd ridden along with my dad in his 18-wheeler once. He usually slept in truck stops, but with me he'd gotten motel rooms. This was just an empty room, but it felt strange to use a place for casual sex that I associated with childhood memories.

Once inside the room, I set down my purse on the floral fabric chair.

Colin reached out and trailed his finger along my jaw. His eyes, almost black in the dark motel room, searched my own. I thought he was going to fuck me then, but he said, "I'm going to make coffee."

I blinked. Shit, coffee. "Okay."

He went to work at the coffeemaker. Unsure of what to do, I sat down in the chair, clutching my purse in my lap like I was waiting for a doctor's appointment instead of rough, dirty sex.

He poured a cup of coffee, adding the cream and

sugar without comment, and handed it to me. I took a few sips. It soothed some of the skittishness I hadn't realized I had. He didn't take any for himself.

Enough of this.

I set down the cup on the cracked countertop and stood to kiss him. I started off light, teasing, hoping to inflame him. This was all calculated, a game of risk and power.

He kissed me back softly, gently, like he didn't know we'd started playing. He held his body still, but his mouth roamed over mine, skimming and tasting.

It wasn't a magical kiss. Angels didn't sing, and nothing caught fire. But he wasn't too rough or too wet or too anything, and for me it was perfection.

I rubbed against him, undulating to a rhythm born of practice. His hands came up, one to cup my face, the other around my body.

I sighed.

He walked me backward, and we made out against the round fake-wood table, his hands running over my sides, my back. Avoiding the good parts like we were two horny teenagers in our parents' basements, new to this. I shuddered at the thought. This was all wrong. His hands were too light. I was half under him already, my hips cradling his, so I surged up and nipped at his lip. Predictably his body jerked, and he thrust his hips down onto me.

Yes. That's what I need. I softened my body, surrendering to him.

"Bed," he murmured against my lips.

We stripped at the same time, both eager. I wanted to see his body, to witness what he offered me, but it was dark in the room. Then he kissed me back onto the bed, and there was no more time to wonder. The cheap bedspread was rough and cool against my skin. His hands stroked over my breasts and then played gently with my nipples.

My body responded, turning liquid, but something was wrong.

I'd had this problem before. Not everyone wanted to play rough, but I was surprised that I'd misread him. His muscles were hard, the pads of his fingers were calloused. I didn't know how he could touch me so softly. Everything about him screamed that he could hurt me, so why didn't he?

I wanted him to have his nasty way with me, but every sweet caress destroyed the illusion. My fantasy was to let him do whatever he wanted with me, but not this.

"Harder," I said. "I need it harder."

Instead his hands gentled. The one that had been holding my breast traced the curve around and under.

I groaned in frustration. "What's wrong?"

He reached down, still breathing heavily, and pressed a finger lightly to my cunt, then stroked upward through the moisture. I gasped, rocking my hips to follow his finger.

"You like this," he said.

Yes, I liked it. I was undeniably aroused but too

aware. I needed the emptiness of being taken. "I like it better rough."

Colin frowned. My eyes widened at the ferocity of his expression.

In one smooth motion he flipped me onto my stomach. I lost my breath from the surprise and impact. His left hand slid under my body between my legs and cupped me. His right hand fisted in my hair, pulling my head back. His erection throbbed beside my ass in promise. I wanted to beg him to fuck me, but all I could do was gasp. He didn't need to be told, though, and ground against me, using my hair as a handle.

That small pain on my scalp was perfection, sharp and sweet. Numbness spread through me, as did relief.

The pain dimmed. My arousal did too, but that was okay. I was only vaguely aware of him continuing to work my body from behind.

I went somewhere else in my mind. I'd stay that way all night.

At least that's what usually happened. Not this time. Instead I felt light strokes on my hair, my arms, my back. His cock pulsed hot against my thigh, but he didn't try to put it inside me, not in any of the places it would almost fit. His hands on me didn't even feel sexual. He petted me, and I arched into his caress.

"Why did you stop?" I meant it to come out demanding, but instead I sounded weak. I hated sounding weak, especially about sex. He may be the one with the cock and the fists, but I called the shots. I had to.

"Allie, shhh. It's okay." He was trying to soothe me, and it was working. He turned me back over and began to kiss me, still murmuring words against my lips. "I'll give it to you. Don't worry. Relax." More words than he'd spoken all night.

I was lost, my emotions all jumbled up from my arousal and my high and subsequent low, at the mercy of this stranger.

What's happening to me? I needed to get back to something I knew. I wanted him to fuck me, to be inside me, to center me. I whimpered, hoping he'd understand.

"Shhh." He arranged my arms and legs so that they were splayed open on the bed and then kissed his way down my stomach. I shifted restlessly, knowing what he planned to do.

I didn't want to say no, exactly, but I couldn't look forward to it. That would probably have sounded weird to some people, that I would have rather gone down on a guy than have him go down on me.

Giving head was a no-brainer for me. I loved cocks, the way they tasted and felt in my mouth. And just the invasion of it, the submission. It was a pretty gross thing to do when I thought about it. Maybe that's why women didn't like blowjobs, but they didn't understand about the power.

Colin, however, settled down between my open legs like he planned to stay. I felt too self-conscious to say anything at all, especially while he was focused on such an intimate place. I couldn't help but tense up.

He kissed the inside of my thigh, his fingers trailing the path of his mouth. He switched to the other thigh, and only when my hips tilted up slightly did he move closer to my center. He licked through my folds, the soft contact startling. His fingers played there too, but he didn't ram his fingers inside me or press my clit. He just licked and suckled and dipped his tongue inside to lap at the wetness pooling there.

It was almost like he wasn't trying to get me to come. In my experience a guy would aim for the good parts and try to get me off as fast as possible, if he even bothered. But Colin licked me like he had all the time in the world. He wasn't speeding up or pushing me on.

The room was silent except for the wet sounds from his mouth on me. The pressure of having to perform an orgasm eased with his leisurely pace. He didn't seem to be expecting me to come now, so it was okay that I didn't. I relaxed into the pleasure, luxuriating in this new sort of worship. God, was this why women loved getting oral sex?

Liquid released from inside me and slid out onto his tongue. He moaned. He actually moaned like…I don't know, like it tasted good. As if the taste of me had turned him on. Damn, that turned me on right back.

For all that I liked giving head, I'd never thought a man could really want to do it to me. He wouldn't like the taste or his tongue would get tired or he'd get bored, but Colin didn't seem to be thinking any of those things. The slow, languid way he licked me again and again spoke of someone who was enjoying himself.

And then, without me having to fake it, my hips rocked in a thrusting motion. He hadn't sped up, but the sensations of his mouth and his own appreciation of the act propelled me toward orgasm. I didn't want it to end.

Colin read my body's pleas and moved his mouth up to my clit. He sucked and slid his finger inside me, using the rhythm of my hips as a guide. So damned good. I couldn't help the moans that came out of my mouth. I'd heard the phrase "I'd die if he stopped," and I'd never understood it before now. I wouldn't have died if he'd stopped, but I just might have cried.

I'd had sex lots of times, but I'd never had a lover so in tune with what my body wanted. It was a conversation, one my mind was barely aware of, but my body knew instinctively.

He played me like he already knew me. He didn't tease me, not withholding my climax or any of that tantric shit, for which I might have had to kill him. But neither did he rush me toward climax. It was as if his entire purpose had narrowed to drawing out my moans.

My whole body went taut, muscles tight, hips flexed up to push against his mouth. My inner muscles clenched at his fingers, pulling them deeper. My breath stopped, and all I could do was make a choking sound. I came and came and came; all I could think was that I'd found something I'd lost.

Colin stroked me through my climax. I jerked violently when his tongue flicked over my clit one last time, and he withdrew his fingers. I expected him to put his cock inside me. Instead he climbed up my body and lay beside me.

He wasn't going to do it.

I felt vulnerable right then, and he knew it. He was going to try to be honorable or something. I didn't want that. I couldn't believe in it.

His cock looked dark and thick and wet at the tip. Something softened in a deep, cold place inside my chest that he was willing to postpone his pleasure for my ridiculous personal shit. That he would even *know* I had any personal shit when this was just a random hookup.

But no, I wanted to please him. He let me push him fully onto his back. I climbed over him and teased him into an openmouthed kiss, ran my hands down his chest. I wanted to give him something, and this was all I had to give.

I'd thought he wanted to be submissive to me, from his gentleness, the way he had worshipped me during oral sex, and the way he was pliant when I pushed him over. It wasn't a role I'd have thought I'd like, but I found myself willing to go there for him. I already knew I'd go down on him. I was looking forward to blowing his mind, along with his cock.

But as I started trailing my kisses downward, my intention clear, he stopped me and shook his head slightly. I'd never had a man turn down a blowjob before. I'd never heard of it happening, not during sex, not when it was free. It flustered me, the way he could do anything to me but he chose to make me feel good.

He arranged me again, so that I was straddling his hips with my legs on either side of him, resting my hands on his chest. His arousal bobbed up toward my hanging breasts.

Colin reached across the bed to his jeans and pulled a condom out of his wallet. He slipped it on and maneuvered my hips onto his erection, then down, slowly. The tautness of his face spoke of urgency, but he held my hips still. We were on his time.

At last he rocked up with tiny thrusts. When I caught the rhythm on my own, he released my hips and smoothed one hand back along my ass. The other came up to my breasts, stroking them, tweaking them.

I could feel the difference in his touch from before. He wasn't trying to get me off now. He was playing with me for his own pleasure. I leaned into his touch, and he sucked my nipple into his mouth.

My arousal built, taunting me, and I tried to speed up.

His hand tightened on my ass. *No, not yet.*

I relaxed into the rocking motion as the pleasure between my legs grew. This was nothing like the sex I'd had before. It was more like a dance or even a meditation. I had no idea how much time passed, but when my legs got sore and tingly, he rolled us over.

He surged into me deeper, in an aggressive rhythm that took me faster and harder. I pulled my legs higher and curled my hands lightly on his neck, opening my body in supplication. I wasn't an active participant any longer. I couldn't help him or even react—I could only take it.

I came again, and this time it wasn't in a blinding explosion but a soft wave. Not a crest but a hum of pleasure, accented with each of his thrusts.

He buried his face into the side of my neck, groaning roughly as he came. His whole body rumbled at the sound, shuddered at his release. His arms tightened their hold on my body, and his hips pushed down into me, harder, deeper—*yes.*

He collapsed and rolled off me. He lay faceup, eyes closed, breathing hard. Colin looked beautiful to me, then. I might have thought he was handsome before, or maybe not, but it was an objective sort of observation. Looking at him now, knowing him—it was too much.

I stumbled off the bed and into the bathroom. I felt my own wetness sticky on the insides of my thighs, but I didn't bother to wash. I sat down on the linoleum and leaned my back against the bathtub, trying to get it together.

I'd thought his sweetness was weak, but that wasn't true at all. He was entirely in control, treating me the way he wanted, not the way I asked for it. And more than that, he seemed to know what I needed, giving it to me despite myself.

He walked into the bathroom, still naked, and sat next to me on the cold floor. I thought it was pretty silly and not totally clean. He put his arm around me and wiped away the tears I wanted to hide. I cried quietly for who knows how long while he held me.

I knew I'd feel stupid when I came back to reality, so I held it off as long as I could. Even after I stopped crying, I kept my eyes closed and buried myself into his side.

Then his stomach growled. We wouldn't be able to sit here forever.

I peeked at him. I wasn't sure what to expect, but it wouldn't be good. Anger maybe, or frustration, disgust, pity, or any number of bad things might be there, before he got the hell out of Dodge.

Instead his lips quirked up into a wry smile. "I'd like to see you again, but this doesn't bode well for my chances."

I laughed, the sound loud in the small space, because it wasn't at all what I'd expected. It could have just been my postorgasm, postbreakdown hormones talking, but if I were honest with myself, I was already falling for him.

That didn't matter, because I had other considerations. One, mostly, but she was enough.

"I like you," I hedged. The disappointment that flickered in his eyes said he read my tone correctly. "But I don't think so."

He considered me for a moment. "Okay," he said. "That's not what we're here for, so I won't push."

He got up and offered me his hand. In the bedroom he handed me my clothes in between putting on his own. I averted my eyes, not because I didn't want to see, but because there was a formality between us now that we'd had sex but weren't going to see each other again.

"I'll drop the key off at the front," he said. "You can finish up in here."

"Okay."

He turned back at the door. "Listen, I own the Oasis Grill down on Kirby, okay? In case you change your mind. Just ask for me."

He paused and then added, "Colin."

I hadn't forgotten.

"Maybe," I said with a noncommittal smile.

"Bye, Allie. Take care."

I peered through the blinds and watched his truck leave the parking lot. So, that was that. Why did I feel a lingering sense of loss? He was a stranger to me. He had to stay that way. That's what this night was for—dirty, emotionless sex. Though this night had been distinctly less dirty and far less emotionless than I liked.

CHAPTER THREE

I LEFT THE motel room, my mind blissfully blank as I drove through the sleepy Chicago streets. My apartment building loomed up ahead, its gray stucco walls and barred windows making it look more like a jail than a home. In Stone Park, that was an amenity. *Don't bother breaking in,* it said. *You won't find anything valuable.*

Within the white walls of my apartment, I took a quick shower to rid myself of the smoky stench of the clubs and the musky smell of sex. I didn't mind them, at least not tonight, but I didn't allow any remnants of my monthly date nights to seep into my regular life. Colin included.

I changed into my standard uniform, sweatpants and a tee. My flip-flops slapped the concrete stairs as I ran up to the identical apartment above mine.

Shelly answered the door. Her hair and makeup were done, though she wore jeans and a tank top. She had an appointment after this.

"So. How was your date?" The lilt in her voice made everything sound ironic, though in this case, the word *date* certainly was.

I hummed in response as I followed her into the living room and flopped down beside her on the couch. I accepted the ice-cream pint and spoon she offered.

"Uh-oh," she said. "What happened this time?"

"I didn't say anything happened." I took a bite. "This is chocolate. How can you eat chocolate this late? It'll keep you up."

"Don't change the subject. Spill."

I sighed and took another bite. "This guy. He wasn't like the others."

"What does that mean?"

"It means, he was…gentle."

"Oh," she said, knowing. "You should let me hook you up."

I shot her a dark look over the spoon.

"I'm just saying. If you're only in it for the sex, you might as well get paid. You can even charge extra to get roughed up."

"Right, so I can get put in jail for solicitation. No, thank you."

She rolled her eyes. "That doesn't happen. Hardly ever."

"We're not having this conversation." I didn't judge Shelly for what she did. I admired her strength. But I had to draw the line somewhere. Right now I was just a regular single mom with her rare date nights. If things got a little heated, who was to know? But accepting payment would change the score. Right now I was in control.

Or I usually was.

I passed the carton of ice cream back to her. "Besides, it wasn't exactly…"

It wasn't exactly bad. It had been amazing. *Real,* my mind whispered. That was what real sex was supposed to be like. It had been anything but bad.

"Allie?"

I looked up and found her watching me.

I smiled briefly. "Sorry. I'm a little distracted."

"I can see that. Curiouser and curiouser." Shelly liked to quote *Alice in Wonderland* to me. It was our secret joke, one I never quite appreciated.

"Don't be dramatic. It wasn't completely lame. That's all."

"I see." The teasing light extinguished from her eyes. "Allison, we have to talk."

Nothing good ever came from hearing my full name. "Bailey?"

"No, she's fine. But…it's related."

A knot formed in my stomach, threatening to expel the churning mixture of chocolate ice cream and alcohol.

"He called me," Shelly said. She was watching me, probably wondering how I would react. I wondered the same thing. I had the expected feelings: fear, revulsion. But maybe relief too, that the paralyzing wait had come to an end. "He said he just wanted to catch up. And…he asked about you. I told him I didn't know where you were."

"How did he find you?"

"Same number since high school." She put up her hands. *I'm sorry.* "Changing numbers is not a good business move for me. Still, I think we may have taken the hiding-in-plain-sight idea a little too far."

"I'm not hiding."

She raised her eyebrows.

"I'm not doing it well," I admitted. "He was the one who left."

Shelly didn't press me, thank God. We walked into her bedroom, where Bailey slept in the middle of the queen-size bed wrapped in fuzzy pajamas, her little fist against her mouth. I scooped my baby girl up, huffing a breath under the weight. Well, she'd be two years old in a few short months, not exactly a baby anymore.

Turning sideways through the bedroom doorway, I left Shelly's place and carried Bailey down to our apartment, depositing her in her own secondhand princess bed. Already in her pajamas, she slept on as I tucked her in under the sheet. I gave her a kiss on the forehead and paused to breathe in her scent. That turned out to be a mistake, because she chose that moment to wake. I calmed her as she fussed, singing my small retinue of nursery rhymes until my voice had gone hoarse and her eyelids stopped fluttering.

This was how I protected her, by keeping the darkness separate.

I couldn't give her a mother who was whole, unbroken. But I could be here for her, night after night, day after day. And if I went on an occasional date night, if there was a twisted side of me let out only then, she never had to know.

I padded into my own bedroom, convinced I'd made

the right choice in not seeing Colin again. Men had one use in my life, and that was what the club was for. I wasn't in a good place for anything more than that, would probably never be.

Colin seemed like a nice guy, not like my usual dates. But I'd been wrong about a man before, hadn't I? So I'd made the right choice. Almost definitely.

When I lay down in bed, though, I thought back to the way he'd been with me, the way he had touched me. The way he had *licked* me. Jesus.

Most kids loved getting presents, but I hated it. After every present people would look at me expectantly, waiting for the gasp of surprise, the exclamation of how much I adored it, and the obligatory hugs all around. I worked at these happy displays, and if it wasn't up to par, I suffered the disappointment. It got to where receiving presents was associated with letting people down.

If a man gave me oral sex, I felt pressure to come quickly. Then it would be like I owed it to him to be properly grateful afterward. Even if I could get off, the stress wasn't worth it. And sometimes I couldn't even come. How could I relax with a stranger's teeth at my most vulnerable place? It wasn't a common problem for me, though, because picking up random guys at bars isn't usually conducive to finding generous lovers.

Colin had licked me, though, and it had been amazing. I had the oddest thought that I wanted him to do it again. That wouldn't happen, of course. But I slipped my fingers into my panties and dreamed.

Chapter Four

I STARTED LOOKING over my shoulder in parking lots, bundled into my thick jacket as if it were armor. Slowing down as I approached alleyways as if something might jump out at me.

Bailey wasn't excused from my insanity either. I crept into her room multiple times a night, making sure she was there and breathing. I even gave in a few times to sleeping on the floor near her bed, sharing the dim comfort of the night-light.

Colin was to blame, of course.

Shelly said it was Andrew—the call from him—but I didn't want to think he could still affect me like this. After all, we were safe from him. As safe as a woman and a baby could ever be from a man who wouldn't wish them well.

I told myself this was something far more basic. More base.

It had been a little over a month since I'd met Colin—since I'd fucked him. I had told Colin what I needed, how I needed it, and he had refused. He hadn't misunderstood—the brief display of force he'd shown when he flipped me over had disproved that possibility.

There was no doubt he was strong enough, but he'd been gentle, kind, almost…loving.

That's not what sex was about for me. Not anymore.

As Bailey and I entered Shelly's apartment, Shelly glanced at me with that blank expression she usually reserved for her johns and then peered back out her blinds. The boarded-up street front was hardly a pretty view. Besides, in our neighborhood, it was best to stay away from the windows.

"What's up?" I asked.

"That car," she said. "I don't suppose you recognize it."

I sat Bailey in the middle of the room, where it'd take her at least a full minute to get up to any trouble, and peeked between the slats. A dark car, probably black, sat out on the street that formed a T with ours, facing our apartment building. I squinted. Between the distance and the glare on the glass, I couldn't tell whether those shapes were passengers or merely seats.

"No," I said. "Why?"

"I saw it there last night. Kind of odd. When I got back from the store this morning, it wasn't there. Now it's back."

It could be anything out on the street. I wasn't sure why this particular car spooked her, except that it did look rather shiny—as in clean—for this area. And though I couldn't quite tell from the shape of it, it seemed somewhat new. Nice cars in a bad neighborhood spelled trouble.

"It's probably nothing," I said. "Or the neighbor in 6A. He's got shifty eyes."

"Yeah," she agreed. "Probably nothing."

It looked like I'd rubbed off on even Shelly. I didn't like seeing her shaken—that wasn't her—so I went for distraction. "Bailey has a new trick."

"Oh?" she asked, some of the scary flatness fading from her eyes.

"Bailey, catch." I gently tossed the large, soft ball to her. She pounced on the ball as it hit the floor, accurately guessing the arc if not quite catching it midair yet.

"Yay!" Shelly clapped. "Who's my good girl?"

Bailey giggled. Previously we had only played roll, so this was a whole new world for her. I left them to their new game so I could change and get to work.

✧ ✧ ✧

THE BAKERY WAS a study in facades, the front of the shopping-strip building all brick, with fancy porticos and signage. Back in the employee parking lot, the cement was exposed, shorter than the brick wall. The contrast reminded me of a movie-set prop.

The inside was split too. The front room, where the customers came in, was spacious and tiled and clean. The back rooms were unfinished, the innards of the building exposed and cramped. Between the two, it was fitting that I was in the back. It wasn't pleasant, just where I belonged.

When I went inside, my coworker and slacker supreme lounged against the counter. I forced myself to smile at him as I clocked in. "Hey, Jeremy."

He glanced at me—my mouth, not my eyes—and then away. "Hi, Allie."

"So…what have you got for me?"

"Two wedding cakes in the freezer. Cupcakes on a timer. Rick took an order for tomorrow."

"Shit, tomorrow? What for?"

"Don't know," he mumbled, staring intently at the refrigerator beside me.

I managed a weak smile. "All right. I'd better get started."

He shrugged and went into the bathroom. His shift was up when I got in, so it'd be on me to make whatever order Rick had agreed to.

After washing my hands and checking on the cupcakes, I went in search of Rick. He looked up from his paperwork. Not bothering with his customer smile, he said, "We got an order for a birthday cake. Fifty people. Over-the-hill theme. Tomorrow."

"Jesus, Rick."

"Don't start with me. This is business." Yes, business. The business where I cooked the cake using my recipes, decorated using my ideas, and took home a barely legal hourly wage. I wasn't too bitter about that, but I didn't want to work overtime on top of it. Not when Bailey was home with Shelly, and Shelly needed me back so she could go to work and make much more money selling her body.

Meanwhile the Sweet Spot was billed as an authentic family bakery with an eye on modern trends. No, Rick wasn't my family. And judging by the covert looks he'd steal when he thought I wasn't looking, he didn't think of me that way either. But he didn't touch me, and that made this better than Shelly's job. Maybe.

"Fine," I said. "Is that all they said?"

"She wants it classy." He rolled his eyes.

I smiled slightly, commiserating. "Right. Over-the-hill, fifty people, classy. Got it."

The back was empty, bathroom door open, so Jeremy had already left. I got to work on the cake batter. In reality the decorating was the easy part. The painful part would be all the waiting that would happen while baking, then cooling, then the first coat, then the full-on decorating. I'd have to work past my shift today to get it done, for sure. Most likely I'd stay up late tonight, rolling out fondant pieces on my counter at home so I could apply them to the finished cake tomorrow.

I barely heard Rick's yell over the whir of the electric mixer. I flipped it off and listened.

"Allie. Phone!"

Only Shelly had this number; only Shelly would care to call. Well, I had to talk to her anyways, ask her if she could watch Bailey late today. Wiping my hands on my apron, I grabbed the plastic receiver.

"Shelly?"

Silence.

"Hello?"

I looked at the phone, then put it to my ear. Still nothing. I hung up. Poking my head out onto the floor, I called to Rick, "Nobody there."

He looked up. "What?"

"There was nobody on the phone. Was it Shelly?"

"It was a guy." Rick shrugged and looked back down at his work. "Asked for you by name."

"Huh." Weird. My dad? Not likely.

My heart still beat too fast, thumping erratically as if my body couldn't make up its mind whether to squeal like a teenage girl or to worry like the woman it had become.

I called Shelly just to check. It hadn't been her, but she agreed to watch Bailey late tonight. Only after I hung up did I think about using Call Return to call the guy back. Not that it was a big deal. Guys weren't exactly standing in line to talk to me.

That's what I kept telling myself. At least until I dropped the entire tray of frosted cupcakes on the floor. *Count backward from ten. Everything will be fine.*

CHAPTER FIVE

BY THAT NIGHT I was practically climbing out of my skin. I needed the release that my monthly date nights provided. They were rough, dirty, and more than a little unsafe—but they were on my terms. Without my fix I felt panicked and jumpy.

It must have showed, because Shelly took one look at me and told me to drop Bailey back off before her bedtime. I said no and took Bailey to the park, then to the library, anything to distract us both from the anxiety that threatened to tear me apart. In the end I gave in, tucking Bailey into Shelly's bed and singing her to sleep before heading out to the club.

As I entered the building, the stench of stale alcohol and sweat hit me. I took a deep breath, a drag. Unsteady on my heels, I wove through the crowd toward the bar. Without planning it, I ended up where Colin had sat last time, and I felt an irrational pang of disappointment to find the bar stool empty. I sat there instead, my ass where his had been, nostalgic over some dirty, cracked plastic.

I signaled the bartender for my usual, but it burned on the way down. I glanced around, feeling cornered, even though I was right in the middle. Everything—the bar, the people, the strobing lights—was covered with a film of grime and dirt and shame. No, that didn't make sense. It was me.

A hard body pressed against me from behind. Some part of my brain flickered with hope that it was Colin. But the body pressed harder, grinding its erection into my back, and I knew it wasn't him. Not that I could recognize his cock print, just that it was too cheesy of a move for him. Too aggressive.

The acrid scent of sweat wafted from behind me. I started to turn, but hands clasped around my waist and squeezed.

"Where do you think you're going?" a rasping voice whispered in my ear. Cold lips slid down the side of my neck, leaving a trail of wetness like a slug.

I shivered. He chuckled.

At the other end of the bar the bartender was serving a group. If I screamed, he would probably hear me, even over the racket of music. He'd help, maybe.

"It's okay, baby. I'm not going to hurt you." *A lie.* My skin prickled in warning. I wanted someone who could be mean, but I tried not to cross the line into outright crazy, and this guy was ringing all the warning bells. His hands were already so tight on my hips that they'd leave bruises. Without having seen his eyes, I knew they would be empty, lifeless. He would be more than rough—he'd be brutal, dangerous.

"Come outside and play," he said.

This was what I'd come for, but now that it was here,

I didn't want it.

"No."

He yanked on my arm, and I toppled from the stool. I finally got a look at him. I looked up to angry eyes and a shaved head. His bulging stomach did nothing to negate the meaty muscle everywhere else.

His eyes looked like I'd envisioned, but with something else: a cruel amusement. Oh, he'd hurt me, all right, and he'd enjoy it. Chills raced through me.

He grabbed my arm and turned to leave, but the bartender called us back. "Hey, stop."

The man paused and turned. "What's up?" he said.

The bartender looked from me, to the guy holding me, then back at me. "You okay?"

I don't want this. Help me. "No, I..." Fingers tightened on my arm, cutting into the flesh. I cleared my throat against the thickness. "I'm okay."

The bartender narrowed his eyes; then he was gone, lost in the swirl of flesh and nylon as I was dragged through the crowd and out the door. The man pulled me over to the side of a building, toward an overflow parking lot, mostly vacant. The heavy beat of the music boomed even outside the club, but I could still hear my blood rushing through my ears. I struggled, but it didn't slow him down.

A truck was parked in the corner, against two brick walls.

He shoved me against the truck door, the metal cold against my back. His body pressed into me as his mouth came down on mine. He tasted me, consumed me, pushing his tongue in deep. Thick, harsh hands groped me, squeezing my breasts and grabbing my bare ass beneath my skirt.

"You know you want it, you little slut. Let's see what you got." He yanked my shirt down at the draped neckline, ripping the fabric. The cold winter air kissed my breasts right before his hands grabbed and burned.

Oh God, I was torn. I'd come here for this. I should want this, but I didn't. I wanted to leave. I wanted him to stop touching me. I wanted to curl up and die.

"Don't be a tease." He squeezed hard. I gasped in pain but let him do it. Of course I did. This was what men did, and I was the girl who let them. The sick sense of triumph I felt every time I proved it was absent this time around.

"That's better, baby." He ravaged my body with his mouth and his hands. He was leaving marks on me, marks I knew from experience I would study later with revulsion and fascination.

Someone else kept intruding even as this guy assaulted me. It was Colin's tongue in my mouth, Colin's hand yanking my hair, Colin's cock pushing painfully into my pubic bone. I closed my eyes. Maybe that was the solution. I could get the roughness I craved, but my imagination would make it safe.

Two fingers shoved inside me. Dry. My eyes snapped open. *Not Colin.*

He jammed them deeper, eliciting a whimpered,

"No." I hadn't meant to say that. I told myself I wouldn't say no, not again. It didn't work, just made them angry. He was moving too fast and it hurt too much, but I could already feel myself start to slide into that place—the place where my mind slowed and none of the pain or the shame could touch me.

It didn't matter, because he didn't mind me. He'd do what he wanted. His lips twisted into a smile.

Abruptly he spun me around so that my exposed breasts were smashed against the door of his truck. His body shoved against mine stole my breath away, then more pain, in time with muted grunts from behind me.

Just as quickly there was nothing. No hard cock pushing against me or rough hands restraining me. Disoriented, I pushed off the truck, staggering back.

"…the fuck away from her," I heard. And shit, I knew that voice.

Not Colin turned into an entreaty in my mind. I slowly dragged my gaze up. *No, please, anyone but him.* But of course there he was, looking like he was leading the charge into a fight instead of just witnessing me in all my shameful glory. Maybe other people dream of being naked in front of a crowded theater, but I already knew this moment would be memorialized in my nightmares: me, half-dressed in a dirty parking lot, in front of Colin.

My arms flew to my breasts, covering them in a futile attempt at modesty. My shoulders hunched as if I could curl in on myself. I envied those little pill bugs that could roll up into a ball. But my body didn't come with any built-in armor. There was just my almost nakedness, exposed by men and my own stupidity.

Paralyzed with humiliation, I could only stand there.

"It's not how it looks," said the man. His voice was loud but shaky. If anyone could recognize false bravado, I could. "She wanted it. She was asking for it."

Oh God. I had the most wildly inappropriate urge to laugh. It was true; it was true.

"Colin," I managed to get out. "It's nothing. It's okay."

Colin swung his gaze from the man to me. "Are you hurt?"

"I'm fine." Close enough.

"Come here." He opened his arm, and without thinking I ran to his side.

"Fuck, I didn't know she was with you!" The man was yelling now, almost screaming. "I didn't know. What the fuck? I wouldn't have touched her, I swear. I wasn't going to hurt her."

With his arm around me, I could feel Colin's muscles tense as if he might spring at any moment, but I wanted this to be over. I leaned into him, molding my arms around his chest in an embrace meant to comfort and restrain.

"Please," I whispered.

He glanced down at me, eyes blazing, but said to the man, "Get the fuck out of here."

The man, whose name I hadn't learned, got into his truck and sped out of the parking lot, leaving Colin and me in a haze of exhaust. We stood in that embrace, my bare breasts pressed against his shirt as if it were the two of *us* having an illicit encounter.

He pulled off his shirt, and my fucked-up mind wondered for just a moment if he would pick up where that man had left off. And how crazy I was; I'd let him.

Colin held out his hand with the shirt. I took it from him and slipped it on with a murmured thanks, unable to look him in the eye.

"Allie," he said.

"Just go," I croaked, looking at his shoes.

It was over, but my anxiety had only increased. He wasn't touching me anymore, and I could hardly blame him. I didn't want to touch my dirty skin either. I'd crawl out of it if it were possible. Just leave this dirty body behind and be someone else.

"What the hell were you thinking?" he asked.

Our roles seemed to have reversed, because I couldn't speak. He was supposed to be the quiet one, and I was supposed to act brave. I shook my head.

"I could understand you wanting to do better than me, but why would you pick that fucker over me?"

"It wasn't like…that." Not exactly and not for the reasons he thought.

When I didn't elaborate, he sighed. "Are you sure you're not hurt?"

"No. I'm fine." If I kept saying it, maybe it would be true. But my breath was coming more rapidly. "I just want to leave, okay? Just go."

"Allie, stop."

"I said go. Leave me alone. I know you want to, so do it!" My words bounced off the brick walls, making his seem unnaturally quiet.

"I'm not leaving you."

Unable to face the intensity of his stare, I looked down, only to feel a warm, strong body encase me. I stiffened only a moment before relaxing into his arms, because I could only fight myself for so long. *Safe.* His chest hair tickled my face, but I rubbed my cheek across it like a cat leaving her scent.

After a few minutes Colin led me to his truck and bundled me in like I did for Bailey, snug and secure. We left the club and my car behind, driving toward my apartment without me having to give directions. The light from the streetlamps only served to make the dark roads more intimate, as if we were the only ones in the city.

It was the perfect mood for confessions, not that I wanted to make any. "How did you know where to find me?"

"The bartender."

I pondered that for a minute. "That guy. The one who… He seemed really scared of you."

A pause. "He just didn't want any trouble."

"It kind of seemed like he knew you."

He shrugged, keeping his eyes on the road. "I'm a mean son of a bitch."

"You're not mean, Colin. You're a good guy."

He smiled faintly. We drove the rest of the way in silence. Despite its inauspicious ending, the whole encounter accomplished what I'd needed. I felt relaxed, sleepy almost.

Even though he'd come home with me, I hadn't expected he would want to have sex. In fact, I would have thought he wouldn't, either out of disgust at what he'd seen earlier or a misguided sense of chivalry.

So I was surprised when Colin led me to my bedroom and kissed me, just a touch of his lips to mine. His hardness pressed against my stomach, announcing his purpose. My feelings were a jumble, but I wanted to give him something. A thank-you, an apology. If there was one thing I knew how to do, it was to let a man fuck me.

He pulled off my clothes carefully, his fingertips pausing at each bruise. I stood for him in the middle of the room, still in my mellow head space. He could have asked me to do anything for him, but what he asked was, "Will I see you again?"

God, please.

How did he do this to me? I'd told myself that men only wanted sex, and that they weren't above using force to get it. And that made a sick sort of sense, because Andrew was a man. A good one, supposedly. One I had trusted, that was for sure. My friend.

When he'd raped me, it was easier to write all men off. The men at the club had only proved the point. They thought they were using me, but it was the other way around. Every slap, every insult, every pinch-of-pain thrust had only cemented the walls that had allowed me to move past the rape and live my life. Now Colin wanted to bring all that down.

I couldn't go back to that dark place in my mind. I'd do anything not to go there again.

So it killed me when I responded, "Yes."

Maybe it made me weak, but I couldn't give him up.

"What?" The little crease in the middle of his forehead showed he was as surprised as me.

"There's something I have to tell you first." I took a deep breath. "I have a kid. A little girl."

"Okay." He drew the word out.

What was the norm in a situation like this? I hadn't dated, hadn't thought about it. "Okay good or okay bad?"

"Okay, I already knew that."

"What? How?"

He shrugged. "Car seat."

I supposed that made sense. And now that I thought about it, there was baby stuff pretty much all over my apartment. More baby furniture than adult furniture. Only my room was spared, because it was empty but for my bed.

"And you're…cool with that?" I asked.

He scowled. "I'm here, aren't I?"

I had my doubts. This whole night seemed like a dream. A strange nightmare-turned-fantasy dream. That guy had been the worst, but then I always expected the worst. What I hadn't expected, what had never happened before, was being saved. Being protected, carried away by a freaking knight in a white truck.

Suddenly I needed a shower. What had been acceptable earlier tonight—that man's hands on me—now felt entirely wrong. Their very imprint defiled me, and by extension Colin.

"I need to shower," I blurted out.

Colin nodded like this pinball of a conversation was completely normal. "I'll be in the kitchen."

I wondered if he'd really be there when I got out. Maybe he'd think about my issues or just the fact that I came with a kid and bolt out the door the second the water started. The thoughts churned my stomach, but if he left, it would be for the best. Definitely for him.

The water shocked my system. *This is really happening,* it berated me, *so stop fucking around.* And I wanted this, wanted Colin, wanted so many things that I didn't have a right to. But no matter how little I deserved it, I could never stop hoping.

I threw on my softest T-shirt and sweatpants and shuffled into the living room, afraid of what I would find. What I found was Colin with practically a party platter at the kitchen table.

Deli meat and cheese, grapes, and crackers decorated a couple of plates. I recognized it all from my fridge, taken out of packages and laid out like this was a soiree instead of a crummy apartment in Stone Park.

"Thought you might be hungry," he said.

My stomach grumbled its agreement. "I have to pick

up Bailey first. My daughter."

"Oh," he said. "Your car is—"

"She's just upstairs," I said. "My friend can take me to get my car tomorrow."

"I'll have someone drive it back. Don't worry."

And for some reason I didn't. Worrying was a well-worn shoe for me, but in the surreal dark of this night I accepted his word. I accepted him. He'd have someone drive it back. I shouldn't worry. I was safe.

Shelly was groggy when she let me in. "How'd it go?" she mumbled.

"Brought a man back."

Her eyes snapped open, full alert. "What?"

She'd been the one to teach me the rules. And by teach, I meant she'd drilled them into me, her lessons replete with stories of women who *hadn't* followed the rules. Even though most everyone at the club held their hookups at their apartments, it wasn't the safe way to play. And considering I had Bailey and also that my dates tended to be assholes of the first order, I played it safe. Relatively speaking.

"Well, he brought me back, technically. I think I'm going to"—what the hell had we agreed to?—"well, to see him again."

Shelly inspected me for a long moment as the suspicion faded from her face and a knowing smile bloomed. "You are, huh?"

"Shut up," I said, though I was more embarrassed than mad. "I didn't agree to marry the guy."

The light of laughter gleamed in her eye. "What's his name?"

"Colin," I grumbled.

She sang under her breath. "Allie and Colin, sitting in a tree…"

"Oh, great. You're in first grade." I marched into the bedroom to fetch Bailey, ignoring Shelly's tinkle of laughter behind me. And continued ignoring her smirk as I passed her on my way out, laden with a sleeping baby girl.

Shelly's soft voice followed me down the stairs before she shut the door. "Then comes Bailey in a baby carriage."

Back in my apartment, I slipped past the kitchen and carried Bailey straight to her bedroom, where she settled immediately. The faded pink toddler bed was old and used, but it had a certain charm. Something old-fashioned and innocent. As soon as I'd seen it at Goodwill, I'd spent too much money on it. It didn't fit with the rest of my sparse apartment, but it fit Bailey.

She was the only thing good and clean in my life. If I had to release the darkness inside me once a month in order to keep it away from her, I had never minded doing so. But now there was Colin, and presumably he would not be okay with me making solitary trips to the club for a quick, dirty fuck. Neither did he want to be rough with me himself. I didn't see how this could work out in the end, but I couldn't bring myself to let him go.

In the kitchen Colin had piled together a sandwich

from the contents of the plates and poured a glass of milk for me. I sat down with this strange, achy feeling. Guilt, maybe. I'd never had someone take care of me like this, not ever. There'd been my dad, but I'd been the one who needed to make dinner if I wanted it done. It was the kind of thing a mother would do, but I'd never had one, at least that I could remember. Who knew Colin could be motherly?

"Thanks." *For everything,* I wanted to say, *not just for the sandwich. Not even for protecting me from the guy at the club. Thank you for seeing my flaws and wanting me anyway.* But those words hung in the air, just out of reach.

"You're welcome," he said, his face blank. He stood up, grabbed my keys from the counter. "I've got to go. I'll make sure your car is back by morning."

He rummaged through a drawer and shoved a piece of paper and pen into my hands. I scribbled my number on the paper and kept my eyes downcast as he plucked it from my fingers.

I was used to feeling competent. In my work and in my life. It wasn't a wonderland, but it was mine. Even the date nights were an extension of that control—they were on my terms. But now I felt bumbling, inept, unable to do basic things like date a guy.

"Hey," I said.

He paused at the door and turned back.

"Maybe we could go out. Tomorrow night," I said.

A faint smile turned his lips. "Sure."

And then he was gone.

I went to the closed door and turned the lock, then rested my forehead against the glossy white paint.

Shelly's voice rang in my ear. *"Allie and Colin, sitting in a tree…"*

Of course, Shelly had it wrong. Even if I were serious about Colin—and we were a far cry from that—I had a baby first. Another man's baby, at that. And love and marriage had nothing to do with this thing between Colin and me. It was sex and companionship. Friendship, maybe. Love was for suckers.

Chapter Six

"How are you?" Colin's eyes raked over my breasts as if checking to see whether any bruises from last night lingered.

Flowers. He was holding flowers. I accepted them, trying to look as if I'd done that before when I didn't think I'd even held a bouquet before. They were heavier than I expected. The smell of damp spring serenaded me.

"I'm okay. Thank you." I led him to the kitchen to hide my blush. "But I…I was hoping to talk to you about last night."

A muscle ticked in his jaw as he leaned his hip against the counter. "Go ahead."

"I know how it looked, but it wasn't like that." Maybe it would have been better to let him believe it was rape, to never talk about it again, but I couldn't bind him to me by pretending to be the victim.

"I heard you say no," he said.

I wiped my palms on the plasticky fabric of my dress. "I know I said that. But sometimes that's what I want. For someone not to stop. I know that sounds kind of crazy. I mean, it probably is crazy. I guess what I'm trying to tell you is that I…have issues."

His face softened just a fraction. "I know. Can you tell me?"

My throat tightened. Actually, every muscle went taut as if the strength of my body could keep my mind from saying too much. It wasn't a choice, not talking about what happened. It was a physical impossibility. It always had been.

People seemed to think they could fix anything by talking it out. Afternoon talk shows and therapists and meetings didn't really help people. All they did was provide a forum for them to talk. Assuming a person *could* talk about it.

The only person who really knew what had happened that night was Shelly. And even then she had pieced it together from my babbling and bruises and, later, the positive pregnancy test.

The thought of telling someone, of telling *Colin*, about that night was…unthinkable. If I tried, my mind shut down, blank and helpless.

I didn't know how much time had passed with me frozen, but he pulled me to him. "It's okay," he said. "We all have issues."

I heard Shelly's voice in my ear, quoting the Mad Hatter. *"We're all mad here."*

His hands running along my back unlocked my voice. "Even you?"

He nodded.

My eyes searched his. "What are your issues?"

"That would be cheating."

I couldn't help but smile. His eyes narrowed on my mouth.

He leaned down and pressed a soft, almost chaste kiss to my lips. I felt his lips open, and I opened mine too. But he didn't plunge inside. Instead his lips fastened on my lower lip and tugged.

My eyes fluttered shut. I felt the soft wetness of his tongue, the scratch of his bristle, but oddly the most intimate was the touch of his nose against mine. I breathed in his exhales, and he breathed in mine.

"Promise me you won't go back to the club," he whispered against my mouth.

I kept my eyes shut. It was safer. "Okay."

This was just supposed to be a casual thing, a date or two, but somehow it felt like more with him. He tempted me to want more. He was like the male equivalent of the sirens I'd read about in high school, who promised happiness when disaster loomed.

"Would you do that for me?" I opened my eyes. "Give me what I need?"

He paused, and I knew he'd understood what I meant. The roughness. His eyes gave nothing away. "Maybe," he said.

Chapter Seven

Colin took me to a hole-in-the-wall Italian restaurant for supper, where we split a classic Chicago pizza. The couple who owned the place screamed obscenities at each other, so obviously colored by affection that it made my heart hurt just to hear.

Later, back at my apartment, Colin followed me to my door. I unlocked it, but before I could enter, he pulled me back and kissed me. I remained frozen that way, leaning away from him for only a few seconds before melting. He pressed me into the door, kissing me, covering me. Headlights flashed onto us from a car in the parking lot, and he broke away.

Colin turned the knob and eased the door open, guiding me inside. As soon as we were in, I pulled him over to the couch, unwilling to let this turn into another coffee session. He sat, and I climbed on top of him, straddling his erection through his jeans. The hardness of it was intimidating and thrilling.

As a young girl I thought of a boy's penis as a weakness, a vulnerability that could be exploited by a well-aimed kickball. But now that I was a woman, a cock was a thing of power, something that could give or claim or bruise.

Our mouths met in a kiss, both licking and exploring and biting. The line between taking and being taken blurred. If my stomach revolted at the thought of having sex, with the memory of that other man's hands still crawling on my skin, that only increased my need. I could do this. I'd prove that I could.

I rocked my hips, pushing my clit onto the ridge of his cock.

"Good girl," he murmured against my lips. I froze at both the humiliation and the pleasure of his words, then rode him over his jeans. Our kiss broke off from the force of my thrusts. He pulled off my shirt and bra to bare my breasts before he covered them with his hands.

The pleasure from my clit ricocheted through me. Almost, almost there.

If only I could stop thinking. *Does he want me? Of course he does; I can feel his erection. But any girl would do. If he wanted me, he'd already have fucked me by now. He wouldn't be sitting there, letting me do this. What is he waiting for? Come on, come already. I'm taking forever. He'll get bored, or worse. I'm doing it wrong. I'm not good enough. If you want me, take me. Please take me. Fuck me. Prove that you want me by fucking me.*

A sting on my nipple snapped me back into my body. Colin pinched the other one, and I gasped.

He slapped the side of my hip, the pain making my inner muscles clench. "Don't stop," he ordered.

His mouth replaced his fingers at my breasts, licking

and sucking. I kept riding him. It hurt, what he was doing, but I knew I needed the pain and he seemed to know it too.

I hovered on the brink. Then he bit down, lightly at first and then harder. Too much. It hurt too much. I couldn't take it. My eyes fell shut as I shuddered through my orgasm.

When I became aware again, I was enfolded in his arms, my head resting on his shoulder. I looked up at him, expecting to see smugness or arousal, but instead he looked troubled.

Shit, I'd done something wrong. "I'm sorry."

"For what?"

"For…doing that. It's your turn."

I reached for his zipper, but his hand stayed me. "Wait."

Panic caught in my throat. He didn't want me. My skin crawled with shame.

But I could fix this. I'd make him want me. "Come on, baby. Put your hard cock in my mouth."

I licked my lips, and his fingers tightened around my wrist. "Please," I said. "Give it to me. I'll make it feel good."

I tried to tug my hand away. He opened his fingers one by one. Gratified to have my hand back, I unzipped his jeans. I'd told the truth. Whatever he felt or didn't feel for me, I'd make his cock feel good.

His cock sprung out, hard and eager. I grasped it at the base and pulled. The softness of the skin was always a shock, too soft for something so hard and scary.

Sliding to the floor, I licked the tip, that faint salty flavor a tease for us both.

"Suck it," he said. My eyes flew to his and found them hot and insistent. I smiled. He'd certainly gotten over his reluctance. But I wouldn't gloat. I took his cock into my mouth, slid it on my tongue, and back toward my throat. When I pulled back, my body sucked in a deep breath, knowing breaths wouldn't come freely for a while.

I edged him deeper with each long suck, craving more even while I fought down a gag. This was what I wanted. A cock was made for fucking. Putting it in my mouth wasn't something that came naturally. I didn't have teenage dreams about being tenderly face fucked. But I did it anyway, with relish, because it felt good for him. It's a special kind of gift, debasement.

My jaw ached, but I welcomed the pain—I was pleasing him. I worked him harder with my tongue and lips and hands. His hands came up and grabbed my hair. *Yes.* He pulled me to him as his hips rocked up, less deeply but faster. I opened my mouth wider in acceptance, straining against the stiffness. He came with a grunt, spurting salty warmth into my throat, his hands stroking mindlessly through my hair.

He hadn't yanked my hair or choked me on his cock, but it was still good. I reveled in the sight of his sated expression. All that buildup, not just the blowjob or making out, but even the dinner—all so that I could give him this moment of peace. Without opening his eyes, he reached for me and pulled me up into the crook of his arm. I curled into his side, shutting my eyes against the sight of his soft cock lying outside his jeans, too raw a reminder of what I'd just done.

He sat up and straightened his clothes. I did the same, suddenly wary.

His face turned away, but not before his eyes darkened. "Allie…I have to go soon."

I looked down. "Oh."

"Hey. I just have to take care of some business. Nothing bad." His finger stroked my cheek and lifted my chin back to him. "That was great."

"Yeah?"

"Yeah," he said. "I'll call you later tonight, okay?"

"Okay."

He turned at the door. Pulling me to him with his hand behind my head, he kissed me, lingering. "I'm going to see you again soon," he said against my lips.

My lips curved against his. "Whatever you say."

"Damn straight." But his eyes were twinkling as he shut the door.

This entire night worked for me. I'd had a great time but wasn't ready for the implications of a sleepover. And I got to pick up Bailey while she was still awake, our dinner being so much earlier than a club visit. That may not have been everyone's idea of a great date, but to me it was almost like heaven.

Except for the cough. It was only a small, dry cough

when I picked Bailey up from Shelly's apartment, but it quickly progressed into a full-fledged mortar explosion, complete with phlegmy shrapnel. As if that wasn't scary enough, her fever spiked from a low-grade 99 up to 102 degrees even with medicine.

Shelly had accepted a client since I'd gotten back so early, so I swiped her laptop to hunt online for advice, but all I found were stern call-your-pediatrician directives. Bailey's pediatrician was long gone from the low-cost doctor's office, and now the only option was the twenty-four-hour emergency clinic. She wailed and coughed and then wailed some more. I'd never seen her like this.

By the time I called the emergency clinic, Bailey was in full-fledged banshee mode. The receptionist gave me a scripted, "She should be seen," barely audible over Bailey's shrieks of pain and baby frustration. That meant spending a hundred bucks we didn't have, but I'd pull it from the rent money for now.

Fortunately, the clinic was not at all crowded for a Saturday night. In fact, after the last couple of people were called in, we had the dingy waiting room to ourselves. I filled out the paperwork and settled in to wait for Bailey's name to be called.

The night air had a calming effect on Bailey. If it wasn't for the nasty cough that intermittently racked her small body, she almost seemed well. But we were there already and had paid, and it made more sense to stay and be seen.

I almost didn't notice him. My attention was split between Bailey and the clock. But he stopped right in front of us, and I looked up. Even then I didn't recognize him right away. A big, scary-looking man who'd had the shit beat out of him, that's what I thought. Angry, red welts covered his face. His right eye was swollen and literally taped shut, with what looked like first-aid tape. My arms tightened around Bailey, and then I recognized him—the man from the club, in the parking lot.

The man who'd almost raped/fucked me and had only been stopped by Colin's threats. Apparently he'd picked the wrong girl to mess with this time, because he was wrecked.

Had he followed us here? Would he try to hurt us?

This was a public place, but I knew from personal experience that no place was safe, least of all a hospital. I glanced nervously around the small, empty room of plastic chairs. The receptionist was behind a frosted-glass sliding window. Probably the most I could hope for was that she would call the cops if trouble started. Oh, and we'd have speedy-fast medical aftercare. Great.

I had to get him away from us for Bailey's sake. There was no going along with it this time. I licked my lips, trying to think fast with an armful of sick baby.

He spoke, but only half of his lips moved, the other half busted up. "I'm not going to hurt you, I swear."

Right, that's what people always say when they have no intention of hurting someone.

"I just want to apologize," he said, the last word slurring almost unintelligibly. He shifted his weight between his feet nervously, or maybe just in pain.

I didn't really care, so long as he left us alone. "Okay."

"I didn't mean anything by it."

"Okay. It's okay." I willed him to walk away, begged him with my eyes.

"I hope I didn't hurt you. Are you all right?"

All I could think of was how to get this guy to leave, but I didn't know what he wanted. If anything, he seemed to be getting more worked up. His breathing increased, but not in a menacing way—more like he'd fall down any second.

I glanced at the closed receptionist window again, wondering if we'd need her help for a different kind of emergency. "Umm, you don't seem so good. Are *you* all right?"

He jumped back. "No! I'm fine. I don't want any trouble."

"Okay," I said, more confused than wary at this point. "So…" I trailed off, glancing at the door suggestively.

"Ah! Right. Well, you take care. And again, I'm sorry. Very sorry." He backed away from me to the door as if I might lunge and attack him with the diaper bag. I heard him mumbling apologies even as the door shut behind him. My whole body slackened in relief that he was away from Bailey. She dozed in my arms, fitful from her sickness but otherwise no worse for the wear.

That call was too damn close.

We made it through the actual visit with minimal fussing. The doctor, who performed what appeared to be a cursory exam, said it was probably a virus but sent us home with an oral antibiotic "just in case." By the time I dragged us back home, it was already midnight. Late, but not that bad, considering all that had happened.

Bailey, who had been exhausted on the ride home, decided to wake up with wide eyes after I administered the antibiotic. Meanwhile my lids were closing. Not good.

My throat started to ache, and it felt so cold. I cranked up the heater, already cringing at the thought of our gas bill next month. I set Bailey up with some soft toys in the living room and then collapsed on the floor beside her, watching her play.

I jolted awake to the sound of my phone ringing. I took a quick inventory of Bailey, who seemed to have collected everything that wasn't nailed down and piled it in the middle like a bird's nest.

My hand fumbled for the phone. "Hello?"

"Hey, Allie." A few of my frazzled nerves settled at hearing his voice.

I glanced at the clock and groaned. It felt later than one o'clock. "Hey, you."

"What's wrong?"

I sighed. "It's nothing. Bailey's caught some sort of bug, and I guess I've got it too. She's wide awake, and I'm exhausted." I took a deep breath, in and out.

"That doesn't sound like nothing. What can I do to help?"

"What? Oh, no. We're fine." I rubbed my hand over my eyes, willing myself to stay awake. "I'm sorry. Did you need something?"

"No. I was just calling to... Well, it doesn't matter. But it sounds like you could use a hand."

"Nah, I'll figure something out. I've done it before, you know."

A pause, then, "Can I come over?"

I glanced at Bailey. "Uh, now? It's pretty late..."

"Yeah, I know. I'll just come over, and if I'm getting in the way, you can kick me out, okay?" He hung up.

The phone slipped from my fingers, as if maybe the conversation had been a dream. I drifted in a haze of discomfort as I watched Bailey use a block of Post-it notes as stickers on all the furniture.

Colin had to knock twice before I dragged myself to the door, holding Bailey. He held up a plastic drugstore bag. "I brought meds."

A burst of pleasure at his thoughtfulness was quickly doused by my exhaustion. I took the bag from him and led him into the kitchen.

"Here, I can take her while you do that." He reached out his hands for Bailey, but his eyes were veiled as if he expected me to refuse.

I hesitated for a moment but realized I trusted him more than that tired doctor. I handed her over, awkward because I rarely did so. He was less nervous than I would've thought as he set her on his hip. She gave a token fuss before settling against him.

The picture of him with her made my heart thump. Apparently Colin had a horse-whisperer effect on both girls in the Winters household.

I hid the strange euphoric feeling by dumping the contents of the bag onto the counter. I sorted through the boxes casually as if men brought me gifts of kindness and health every day. "Wow, did you buy out the store?"

"I didn't know what you already had, so I just got everything they had."

I opened a few to take. "You didn't have to do this. Thanks, though. This is really great."

"No problem. Should I put Bailey to bed?"

Bailey examined Colin with undisguised curiosity, looking no closer to sleep than she had a few minutes ago. "Uh, sure. You could try that."

"Any specific thing she likes?"

"I usually read a few books and then sing to her. When she wakes up in the middle of the night, like tonight, I try to cuddle her back to sleep."

"Okay," he said and headed toward the hallway.

No one except for me and Shelly had ever put her to sleep before, and I doubted Colin had tons of childcare experience, so I wasn't expecting success. Still, grateful for the reprieve, I leaned against the counter with my eyes closed for a few minutes.

I took a bunch of pills to help with various symptoms and then headed to Bailey's bedroom. The door was cracked open, and I peeked inside. Bailey lay on the bed with her eyes closed.

Colin sat on the edge stroking her hair and singing. "*In my thoughts I have seen rings of smoke through the trees, and the voices of those who stand looking...*"

Led Zeppelin! I clapped my hand over my mouth.

This big, strong man, wearing a muscle shirt and cargo pants, sang rock songs to a toddler in the middle of the night. I was so toast. Game over. And it was doubly terrifying, considering I had no idea how to make him stick around. He would leave and take his sweetness and his Pepto and our hearts.

CHAPTER EIGHT

IN DISGUST AT my own vulnerability, I stalked into the living room and started picking up Bailey's things. How was I supposed to hold myself emotionally aloof when he was being so damn sweet? But the truth was, he might be a knight in shining armor—but I couldn't be saved. I was too far gone for that. I'd been too far gone since I was sixteen. And now, three years later, I felt ancient.

Colin came in and leaned against the door frame. "Hey, I can do that. You can rest."

"Is she down?"

"Out like a light."

I closed my eyes again for a long minute, savoring the peace. "Thank you. Really."

"No problem."

"Here." I patted the couch. "Come and sit. Not too close, you don't want to catch this thing."

He rolled his eyes and sat. "After what we did earlier, I don't think an extra foot is going to help me."

I laughed, which kicked off a coughing spurt. When it was over, I groaned and rolled my head forward. Colin shifted closer and kneaded my shoulders.

"Jesus," I said. "Stop being perfect."

His hands froze. "I'm not perfect."

"Okay," I said, partly because I hadn't meant to offend him and partly because I wanted him to continue. His fingers, thick and calloused, started to move again, pushing away my knots. Those hands were strong enough to hurt me, but instead they brought me pleasure and now comfort.

God, this was better than sex. It was probably best not to tell him that, male ego being what it was, but it was true.

"So good," I managed to groan, to let him know I appreciated him.

"Shh," he said. Even better.

He rubbed my shoulders, my neck, even my arms, until I relaxed back into him—a puddle of sick, exhausted woman. My mind entered a slushlike state, dreamy. His arms wrapped around me, gently rubbing my hands. Who knew hands had tension?

At first I'd been so desperate for relief that I was content to be pampered, content to use Colin that way. But after a while, even through my fog I felt the oddness of the one-sided flow of pleasure. Normally I would feel guilt that I'd even accepted it, and maybe concern that he would demand recompense, more than I had to give. But with Colin it was different. There wasn't fear, only gratitude. I wanted him to feel good, as good as me. Of course, I also didn't want to move or even open my eyes, so that was a dilemma.

I turned my hands over. My fingers felt small and fragile in his large ones, like a bird's wings fluttering in a cage, but he wasn't holding me down. He let me explore, my fingertips tracing the calluses on his palms. I curved my fingers around to the backs of his hands. Rough skin, though not as rough as the calluses, and the soft hair of a man. My fingers inched up—it was coarse and…? My eyes snapped open, and I looked down to see open cuts on his knuckles. I stared at them for a moment.

An icy shiver ran down my spine, one that had nothing to do with my fever. I didn't know if I was slow because of the late hour or because I didn't want to see it. I remembered what the man at the clinic had said—that was the exact phrase Colin had used last night, that the guy just didn't want any trouble. Last night the guy had acted like he knew Colin, or at least knew *of* him.

I turned slowly in Colin's arms until I was facing him, still clutching his hands. "How did you get these?"

His face closed up, confirming my fears. And in his eyes there was knowledge of what he'd done. There was caution too, which I hated.

"Colin."

He looked like he might not answer me, but he said, "It was nothing. A disagreement."

"Who?"

He shrugged, not casually enough. "Someone where I work."

"Right. Someone didn't pay the tab, so you beat him up?"

Colin shook his head, but his eyes never left mine. "The restaurant isn't the only place I work."

"Tell me." *Tell me you didn't do that to him. Tell me you aren't another violent man.*

"My brother. He owns a few businesses."

"Was it the man from the other night?"

"Why would you think that?"

"Gee, I don't know. Maybe because you tell me you have something to take care of. Then I see him with the shit beat out of him. And then you come around with—"

"You saw him? When the fuck did you see him?"

I flinched at his language, which was laughable considering my own dirty mouth. Still, this one was less like an exclamation and more like a lash.

"Did he come here?" he asked. "I swear to God, I'll kill him."

I pulled away from him and stood, wrapping my arms around my sides. "You did it, then."

"Yes, I kicked his ass, but it was a fair fight." He stood and paced away from me. "What? Did you like him or something?"

"No, I don't *like* him, but I don't want to see him hurt because of me. Jesus, Colin."

"You didn't do it. He started it, and I finished it."

I rolled my eyes. "I am not some stupid girl you fight over, winner take all."

"I wasn't fighting to win you. I was teaching him a lesson. Now answer me. Did he come here?"

"No! Not that I owe you an explanation, but apparently you'll go homicidal if I don't tell you. I saw him at the ER where I took Bailey, okay? All he did was *apologize* to me. And he looked like shit. You seriously hurt him."

"Good. But he shouldn't have talked to you at all. I warned him what would happen if he did."

My eyes widened. "You're not going to do anything else to him."

He said nothing.

"I'm serious. I can't believe you even did that much. This isn't like the caveman days. Who does that? Crazy, violent people, that's who. You could've really hurt him." And then a thought hit me. "You could get in trouble. Even go to *jail*."

"If I do get sent to jail, it won't be for *that*."

"What does *that* mean? What other things are you doing?"

He gave a quick shake of the head. *Don't ask.*

"I swear to God, Colin, do not make me play twenty questions. If you are up to something dangerous and you are bringing it here into my house with my daughter, then I have a right to know."

Finally he looked ruffled, his cheeks pinking and his nostrils flaring slightly. "I'm not bringing anything into your house. No one will hurt you or your daughter, especially not if I'm seeing you."

"Is this supposed to be comforting? Because it's really not. What does that even mean? Who the hell are you? The mob?" I tried to laugh but choked on it when he shrugged.

"Nothing that organized."

I stared at him, dumbstruck. Out of the frying pan and into the fire, that's what had happened.

He sighed. "Can you please sit down?"

"I don't want to sit down."

"Allie. Sit."

I sat.

"You know I own a restaurant. But before that I worked for my brother. I won't lie and say everything was above the table, because it wasn't. It wasn't always legal and it wasn't always...good."

He looked at me resignedly, as if I would condemn him. I thought of Shelly, and I thought of Andrew. My own halo was much tarnished. No, I wouldn't condemn Colin for his past, but that didn't mean I had to accept it into my life. I had to think of Bailey.

"You aren't involved in that stuff now, right? I mean, now that you run your restaurant."

"Most of the time." His words were slow, too carefully chosen to be comforting. "But sometimes he asks for my help, and I do it. That's what I was doing at the club the night we met—meeting him."

"What types of things do you do?"

"Whatever he needs done."

"Violent things?"

"I never claimed to be perfect." His eyes focused on mine, his voice steady.

A small laugh burst out of me, the sharp sound

bouncing off the walls of my bare apartment. "No, you didn't, but there's a long way from not perfect to violent criminal, don't you think?"

He said nothing.

"And if I asked you to stop doing those things, would you?" But I already knew the answer.

"He's my brother."

I wasn't angry. Not angry for whatever slight deception there may have been not to tell me this up front. Not for his past, whatever illegal or violent things he had done. Not even angry for what he had done to the guy from the club.

I was afraid.

Afraid that somehow, that world would intersect with mine, when I'd worked so hard to isolate myself. Even my club nights were carefully orchestrated and contained, incidents that never spilled over into my real life. Until Colin.

I was afraid I'd misjudged him, that he wasn't the nice guy I'd thought him to be. Just doing bad things in your life didn't make you a bad person. I believed that firmly. But how could I tell the difference? I couldn't trust him. I couldn't even trust myself.

"You're breaking up with me, aren't you?" An undercurrent of steel in his voice was the only sign of his displeasure.

"It's not like we're going steady. We've had one date and two fucks. That does not make a relationship."

"Don't bullshit me. You and I both know it was different between us."

I paused, then said more quietly, "Why me? You could go back to that club and pick up a girl who's hotter than me, who doesn't have issues, that's for sure. I need to understand why you want me."

He shook his head, though it wasn't a refusal.

"It's not just the sex. It's…it's this." He waved his hand around my apartment.

Bare white walls, cheap ratty couch, strewn plastic toys. I just looked at him.

"I want you. I want *this*." He gestured between us in frustration, maybe at me for asking the question, maybe at himself for not being able to answer.

"Oh, Colin."

He hid behind a thicker skin than I could ever hope to breach. The only reason I was seeing this was because he'd let me in. I fell in love with him a little right then, as he sat, so large and competent yet so vulnerable. I wanted him for my own, and that wanting was like a chant in my head. A greedy, futile chant.

"Maybe there is something special between us," I finally said, "but it's just too hard. I've got so much baggage I could sink the Titanic, and you…well, you have your own baggage, don't you?"

Maybe I was being mean, I thought, as I watched his defenses tighten up again right in front of my eyes. Sometimes mean was good. Sometimes mean was the difference between survival and going under.

"Don't put this on me, Allie. I'm not the one too

scared to give this a shot."

"No, you're just the one who's part of a violent, tiny mob family who goes around beating people up for fun." We had both raised our voices, angry that this wasn't going to work and yet unable to fix it.

"I can't believe you're mad about that. That guy was an asshole who hurt you. He deserved what he got."

"That's not the point. It's not up to you. Did you ever think of what would happen if he got angry with me and tried to hurt me back? I was at the clinic with Bailey when I saw him."

"I made it clear he wasn't to touch you ever again. Besides, you should have called me if you needed to go to the clinic."

I rolled my eyes. "Oh, please. I'll just call you whenever I need anything at all."

"I would have come with you."

"Yeah, unless you were doing something for your brother."

His nostrils flared, but he didn't respond.

"It seems to me like you're the one who's stuck in the past. If you want to be with me and Bailey, fine. Then stop doing dangerous things that could come back on us."

"You can't ask me to give up my family."

"I'm not asking for that. You can see him all you want, just don't do anything illegal for him, anything violent."

"It's the same thing."

"Then what kind of family is that? He just wants you for what you can do for him."

He stepped toward me. "Yeah. That's right. And you think you're better than him? We all pay for what we want, me included. You're not giving me anything for free, so don't play the martyr. You'll fuck me to get what you want, and who the fuck cares what I want?"

I stared at him in shock.

He lowered his voice, still breathing hard. "Everyone has a price, Allie. And I'm not paying yours."

Colin turned and left the apartment, the door latching quietly behind him.

CHAPTER NINE

"THE ANTS ARE back!" In my frustration I let my voice ring out through the bakery. It was closed at this early hour anyway.

"Jesus Christ," Rick swore from the bathroom.

With a sigh, I wiped away the ants and rolled out my dough.

A few minutes later, Rick came out. "You didn't have to scream at me. Missed the toilet."

"Well, I hope you cleaned it up, because I'm not touching your piss." I waved my flour-covered fingers at him.

He narrowed his eyes at me but returned to the bathroom. A minute later he came out.

"Did you wash your hands?"

"Yes," he snapped but then turned back to the bathroom. I heard the water run for a minute before he came out again.

He leaned against the wall by the phone. "What's up your ass?"

"It's not unreasonable to expect you to wash your hands. Clean working environment. Food preparation. Health code violations. Any of this ring a bell?" Working being a relative term for Rick, but between him and the bugs, this place was getting gross.

He shrugged. "It's not that. You've been bitchy lately."

"This is just how I am."

His expression turned mulish. "Maybe, but it's been really bad for a few weeks now."

"PMS." I gave him my best feral smile. *Drop it.*

"See?" He grinned. "Bitchy."

"Yeah, well, do me a favor and fire me." Not that he would, and not that I really wanted him to. The job sucked, but it kept Bailey in diapers and that was the important thing.

"Mmm, no thank you. Maybe if you don't get that custom cupcake order done by the end of your shift."

"Don't tempt me."

He went into his office, probably afraid he'd actually annoy me enough to bail. I was the only person he trusted enough to do the large, expensive orders. And none of the others even did fondant. If only I could use my leverage for something useful, like a raise.

Bitchy. I snorted. Hell, yes, I was bitchy.

I had literally no idea where my electricity payment was coming from. No, scratch that. I did know. Shelly. She'd offer it, and Bailey couldn't very well live in an apartment with no lights, so I'd accept. Shelly earned that money on her back. If anyone had to turn tricks to support Bailey, it should be me.

As if I wasn't feeling guilty enough, it looked as if

Shelly had a crazy client obsessed with her. The same black car parked on the street at odd hours. One bright day I caught the glare from a camera lens aimed at our apartment building. I ran inside with Bailey, and the car drove away. I considered calling the cops, but we knew they wouldn't do anything. Besides, both Shelly and I had an aversion to cops, though for a slightly different reason.

My "date nights" had gone to shit. And the man who'd done it, well, I'd broken up with him. Or maybe he'd broken up with me. Had we ever been dating? The more time passed, the hazier it became. But I did know that I needed to get fucked.

I could go to the club, but after the last trip I was gun-shy. Some slut I was—amateur.

I'd had a rough couple of weeks. Bitchy was the least I could do.

The detailed construction of gum paste calla lilies distracted me. Rick called out from his office, "Hey, get out of here, kid."

I glanced up—it was fifteen minutes past the end of my shift.

"One sec." I stroked my brush from the inner curl to the tip, leaving a striated peach coloration. Tomorrow I'd paint light pink blush onto the tips. Perfect for the wedding cupcakes they'd adorn. Once the paint dried enough to set it down, I laid the flower on the tray with the others.

The sky had darkened to dusk by the time Rick came

out of his office. "What are you still doing here?"

"Just cleaning up."

"Hey." His hand stopped mine on a package of food coloring. His eyes were missing their usual playful glint. "Are you sure everything's okay?"

I sighed. "Would it be possible for me to get a raise?" He didn't respond right away. "Or maybe just get some extra shifts?"

"Are things that bad?"

"It's just that Bailey had an ER trip a couple of weeks ago, and things are a little tight."

He ran his hand through his hair.

"Never mind," I said. "I'll work it out."

"No, you deserve a raise, but you know things have been slow around here. We're already short on staff just to stay open. But I'll take a look at the books, okay? I'll see what I can do." Maybe the bakery wasn't as busy as it once was, but I'd honestly thought he was just being cheap before. Now I felt greedy, asking more if the bakery was truly struggling. Even if he did find me an extra fifty cents an hour, it wasn't going to solve my cash-flow problems.

"Thanks, Rick. You're a good guy." I was relieved to see the creases ease from his face. Worry didn't look good on him. On a whim I kissed his cheek. He caught my arm as I pulled back.

"You smell like sugar," he murmured. My breath caught. What the hell was he doing?

I tried to laugh. "Everything here smells like sugar."

"I'm glad you told me what the problem was. I'll do what I can, but I wish it was more." *I wish it was enough* was what I heard in his voice. And sadness.

I wasn't sure I could handle the cause of it. Aiming for casual, I leaned back, and he loosened his grip on my arm.

"You do plenty," I said. "Where would I be without this job?"

"Not seeing my sorry ass every day, that's for sure." He turned and went back into his office. His words were light enough but without any real good humor.

Rick could be a jerk sometimes, but mostly he was decent. And happy. After all, a guy who owned a bakery but didn't bake, that was right out of one of Bailey's Dr. Seuss books. But money was tight, and maybe the bakery was in trouble. Colin was right—everyone had problems.

Outside the back door of the bakery, I checked left and right along the alleyway. Empty as usual. I walked along the brick wall, skirting away from the smelly Dumpsters until I reached the employee parking lot. I got in my car and breathed in some air. It was musty but safe.

I drove home on autopilot, shedding the tension of work and worry in anticipation of seeing Bailey. When I got out of the car and headed for the stairs, I had almost forgotten to check my surroundings. Out of habit, I turned my head. And froze.

"Hey, Allie." Andrew leaned against the wall.

That carefree smile. Those sparkling blue eyes. The

face that was as known to me as my own. The one I saw hints of in my daughter, who was right upstairs.

My body, ever the traitor, wanted to turn and run. Get away, it shouted. As if in exclamation, chills rippled through my skin.

But I had to stay and act normal. This was the path I had chosen a very long time ago, faking it. I wasn't even sure what would happen if I ever decided to stray from it. What would honesty in this look like?

"Allie?"

"Andrew." Thank God my voice worked. It had been a crap shoot, really. "What are you doing here?"

"Just visiting an old friend."

My mind formulated insane escape routes more appropriate for an action flick than real life. "Oh, yeah?"

He pushed off from the wall. We were completely out in the open. Sure, no one was actually around, and yes, this neighborhood was shady. But nothing bad was happening. Nothing bad *would* happen. But my body didn't seem to believe that. It was shivering and sweating and clenching like a spastic marionette.

His arms came around me in a bear hug. My face smashed against his chest. I drew in a Andrew-filled breath that soothed me. How could the sight of him terrify me but the smell of him comfort me? My body was as confused as my mind.

His embrace tightened to the point of pain. Abruptly he released me, then pushed past me to my car. I spun around, watching in horror as he peered into my backseat. He looked back at me. "This is yours."

"Yes." He knew my car, of course. He'd been in it before. He'd even helped me fix it up, back in the day.

"No, that." He pointed through the window to the car seat. "You have a baby?" His voice was strained. The first crack in our shared facade.

"Andrew." So many things in that single word: *don't go there, I don't want to tell you, you don't want to know, why did you hurt me?*

But he didn't hear them, or didn't care. "How old is it?"

"Please. Just go."

"Answer the question."

"It's none of your business. There. How about that for an answer?"

"Don't bullshit me. You were never good at it."

"I'm not bullshitting you. That's the truth. Bailey's not your business."

"Bailey." He said it slowly, weighing the name. It made me angry. His eyes faded from anger into wonder. "A girl?"

"She's mine. You have nothing to do with her."

"Really? Is that true?" His tone called me a liar.

I said nothing, just narrowed my eyes at him in impotent rage and fear.

"Tell me who her father is, if not me? Is it Kyle, from third period? You went out once, right? Did you see him again? Or was it that guy where you work? Or are you hooking like Shelly, and you got knocked up? Whose is it, if it's not mine?"

I hated, *hated*, the stinging warmth in my eyes. I blinked, but it only made it worse. Weak. Stupid girl, never learns.

"Let's not fight."

Andrew's voice turned soft, a supplication I'd interpreted as affection back then. Now I wondered whether it had always been a front. Or was it sometimes true? Either way he couldn't be trusted.

"It doesn't have to be like this. We were friends once. I want to be your friend again. I've been looking for you everywhere. And now I find you, and we have a…a kid together. Jesus. It's crazy. I mean, I'm in shock. But it's good, right? You and me, it's always been you and me."

Somehow during his speech he'd moved forward, and I'd moved back until my back was against the wall. "No. I don't want to be friends. I can't do that."

"I know that you're…angry at me." It was the closest he'd come to referencing what had happened that night. "But we can work through it. I know we can."

"I don't want to, don't you get that? If you cared, you wouldn't even ask me."

"You're wrong, Allie. It's because I care about you that I'm here. I made a mistake when I left before. I should have stayed and fought for you, but I've always cared about you. You have to know that."

"It's not going to happen between us, not ever."

"You can't just throw this away. You can't just ignore me because you're angry." His voice was rising now. I hoped Shelly would know to stay inside, to keep her and Bailey out of sight rather than check on me if she heard him. In this neighborhood, staying inside was the default thing to do.

I kept thinking that if I just told him no, in clear terms, that maybe he would walk away. But that was stupid. It hadn't worked before. I tried a new tactic. "She's not your kid. You're right. I got knocked up by some guy I met at the bakery. So don't worry."

"I don't believe you. I told you, you never lied good. She is my kid. I want to see her."

"Just stop." My voice came out so shrill that it shocked me into silence. I took a deep breath. "I swear to God, Andrew, you will not get to see her. I am her mother, and you are not her father. You did not make that baby in any way that counts, and I am not going to let you in our lives. Do you hear me?"

"Yeah," he said. "I hear you."

His words barely registered as I went on. "You will not touch her. You will not touch me, not ever again. Do you understand that? Are you hearing me? Are you listening to me tell you no, because goddammit, Andrew, I said it before and you didn't listen. I need you to hear me now."

He grabbed my wrist and twisted. My whole body followed. The wall stopped me, but I wished it hadn't. I wanted to melt into it, to just fade away. All my hard-fought words of power, obliterated with the grip of his fist.

Where was the boy who'd chased me on the pier or filched my books, only to return them just as stealthily? I wanted to ask him that and so much more, but the cold brick muzzled me. "I do hear you," he said behind my ear. "And I…I want to listen to you."

"But you won't." My shoulders slumped against the wall like a cold embrace.

"It was a mistake to walk away before," he said. "And it was a mistake…what happened. I want to make it right with you. And now, with her. It's a lot to take in, but I feel like I owe her something. And I already know I owe you."

"Why don't you start by letting me go?"

He released me. I rolled against the wall to face him but still leaned against it. It was so blessedly vertical.

"I don't think I can walk away this time," he said.

I was too tired to fight, and I already knew I'd lose. He'd proven that handily. "You wanted to leave, so you left. You want to stay, so you will." *You wanted to fuck me, so you did,* but I didn't say that. "What about what I want?"

"Tell me what you want. Tell me how I can help you."

He didn't get it. He could help me by leaving. But he wouldn't go.

I shook my head. "Go away, Andrew. Go away, or I'll call the cops and they'll make you." It was risky, to bring up the cops. Andrew wouldn't want them involved, would think he might get in trouble if they were called. He didn't know the cops didn't care, but he didn't call my bluff.

"I'll go," he said. "But I'm staying in town. I'm going to give you some time to cool down, think things through. Then we'll talk again. We're going to work this out, whether you believe that right now or not."

Chapter Ten

ONCE HIS CAR was out of sight, I ran up the steps. Shelly took one look at my face, said, "Shit," and pulled me inside. "What happened?"

I walked past her to Bailey, who saw me and held out her arms for me to pick her up. Squeezing her close to me, I buried my face in her downy hair. She gurgled a protest and squirmed.

"You're scaring me," Shelly said. "Tell me what happened. Is it Rick?"

"What? Why would it be Rick?"

"I thought maybe...I don't know. You're just not giving me much to go on. You come back late from work, and now you look like you've seen a ghost."

"I'm sorry I was late." I set Bailey down, and she immediately went back to her toys.

I sat down on Shelly's couch. My fingers stroked the soft leather. It was so out of place in this crappy apartment, but I knew why she was here. It was for me. For Bailey. Oh God, what would I do? She reached for my hands, and I jerked back without thinking.

"Jesus, Allie. Tell me what's going on."

"It's Andrew." I waved my hand. "He was here."

"Where? In Chicago?"

"No, *here*. At our apartment. Just outside. I watched him drive away, but he said he'll be back. He's coming back."

"Oh, shit."

"And he saw Bailey's car seat. He knows about her. I need to go. I need to take her and leave."

"That's crazy. Where will you go?"

"I don't know. Maybe I'll track down my dad. Ride in his truck for a while." It was mostly a joke. My dad may not have been a stellar example of fatherhood, but he'd help me if I were in trouble. Still, riding around in the cab of a semitruck with a baby wasn't a realistic plan.

But what could I do other than run? The law wouldn't be on my side. I'd found that out two years ago.

It would only take a DNA test to confirm what Andrew already suspected. He was the biological father of Bailey. And if he pursued it, he could be her father legally too. At one time I would've thought those were the only ways that counted, but not now.

I didn't think of him as Bailey's father. I couldn't. She was mine.

If I stayed, he could compel me to let him near Bailey. Hell, to let him near *me*. The court system, the authorities, they would support him.

But if I ran, what kind of life would that be for Bailey? When would it end? I had trouble enough keeping her stocked in diapers and secondhand plastic toys even with a reasonably steady job at the bakery. On the run, even that would be in jeopardy, and who would watch Bailey when I worked? I wasn't sure I could hold up without Shelly.

"Hey, there," she said. "I know this is bad, but we'll work it out. You're not in this alone."

"Ah, God." I put my head in my hands. "I'm not trying to be a whiny bitch here, but sometimes it feels like the cards are stacked against us, you know?"

"Yeah," she said. "I know. Do you think...?"

"You know the police won't help. And I don't have money for a lawyer, much less a good one."

"I wasn't going to say that." At her pause I looked up to see Shelly tracing her fingernails in the woodlike grooves of the plastic coffee table. "What about that guy?"

I blinked. "Colin? What about him?"

"Don't say you haven't thought of it."

I hadn't thought of it, but I was now. To send Colin like he was some goon to shake Andrew up. To fuck him up. After all, Colin had already shown a willingness to protect me in the physical capacity. "You're crazy."

She pressed her lips together and refused to look me in the eye.

I shook my head. "No. Freaking. Way."

"Okay, okay," she conceded. "I wasn't saying it was a great plan. Listen, do you want me to talk to him?" And the way she said the word "talk" made it clear what she really meant. Persuade him. Maybe even whore herself out for me.

"Shelly," I said; then I couldn't get any more words past the lump in my throat. I couldn't let her do that. But God, that she would even do something like that for me. For Bailey. She was my daughter. I should be able to protect her, but I couldn't even protect myself.

"Come here, sweetie." She folded me in her arms. Between the two of us, I was the mother. I was responsible for Bailey and myself. And I felt responsible for Shelly too. She was only a few months younger than I, and prettier and probably smarter than me as well. But somehow she'd always trailed after me through middle and high school. I'd always suspected she'd had a crush on Andrew. But when he'd fucked me over, both literally and otherwise, she'd been there to help me. She'd continued to help me all this time, even now offering her body in exchange for what? For friendship? For this pale imitation of a family?

I didn't deserve her loyalty.

Straightening my back, I pulled away from her warmth. "Thanks, Shelly. Don't worry. I'm not going to do anything crazy. He said he'd give me some time, so I'll think of something. Everything will be fine."

Of course she didn't believe it. I didn't either, but she let me go.

I carried Bailey down to our apartment and put her in her high chair. I set down a jar of sweet peas and let Bailey go to town with a plastic spoon. It felt weird to do something as mundane as mealtime when my world was being ripped apart. But that's the thing about kids—they make you practical.

A stronger mom, a better mom, would probably have chastised her for the mess. But it was easier to let her make a mess and then clean it up after. Green mush sprayed across the linoleum floor wiped clean in a single swipe.

If only all my problems could be cleared with such ease.

After Bailey ate, I peeled off her clothes and diaper and carried a pea-spattered baby to the tub. After washing her, I let her sit for a few minutes in the warm water while she splashed around with some foam alphabet letters. To say she was my everything wasn't giving her enough credit. I didn't know how I would have gotten through those dark months back then without her inside me. Even now my composure had all the sturdiness of a house of cards. I'd just as soon lie down and let Andrew have his way with me than fight him again. And Colin. Well, Colin. But always there was Bailey to consider, and so I had to be strong.

Bailey was rough to put down to bed that night, probably feeding off my nervous energy. I sang her all the lullabies in my arsenal three times before her eyes drifted shut.

I took a shower and slipped on a ratty T-shirt. Then paced. I couldn't go anywhere, for obvious reasons, and besides, there was nowhere to go. I considered watching TV, reading a book, but nothing could hold my focus.

My mind ran like a hamster on a wheel.

What a relief it must be for a rape victim to hate her rapist. But even if I hated Andrew, I also loved him. Not the way he'd wanted me to. I loved him as a friend, a brother. It may have been chaste, but it was real. Maybe the most I'd ever loved anyone, at least before Bailey.

And that old love was still inside me like a cancer.

Maybe if I could believe what I'd told myself all those nights at the club, that I didn't really have the right to say no, that all guys were assholes, I could find some kind of peace. Then, at least, what Andrew had done would make sense.

I had thought I was over it. It wasn't even rape, right? Sure I'd said no, but men didn't listen. Now, though, with Colin waiting in the wings, tempting me and respecting my refusal, I had to wonder if I'd just been fooling myself.

And that begged the question—what would it take to truly get over it? Was it even possible? The thought of being broken forever was a scarier thought than anything Andrew could do to my body.

It wasn't the first night I'd baked in lieu of sleep. The methodical measuring of ingredients and the steady rhythm of mixing never failed to soothe me. During the day I played with recipes, taking delight in creating something new. But night baking was about comfort. All I had to do was follow the formula, and everything would turn out okay. Better than okay, considering double chocolate brownies came out of the chasm.

CHAPTER ELEVEN

THE DRIVE ONLY took twenty minutes, as loitering teens and half-empty strip malls gave way to artistic cafés and pocketed neighborhoods. My would-be Prince Charming's castle turned out to be a white, bungalow-style house with a front porch. It was small compared to some of the others, but still much too big for a bachelor. Too domestic.

Colin had called this morning, asking me to come over and talk. I owed him that much. It was more of a meeting than a date. More of a breaking up than an opening.

I told myself that, again, fussing over my meeting-date outfit as I sat in the front seat of my car. But I didn't really believe it. I wanted to make it right with Colin.

The heart wants what it wants, even if that means fucking over the people it loves. Because it really wasn't fair to drag Colin into this. Bad enough I was so messed up, and that I was broke and had a kid and all the other things that were wrong with me. All the things that made me a poor candidate for a girlfriend, as if this were a job interview, an audition.

After the new troubles with Andrew, I should leave Colin well enough alone. It was impossible to say how it would affect him, impossible that it *wouldn't* affect him, indirectly somehow.

Or maybe directly, by me running to him for help, like now.

I fidgeted in the car for ten minutes, parked a bit too far away from the curb as if those extra few inches could keep me from arriving. I caught movement out of the corner of my eye and looked over to see Colin open the front door. I couldn't see his expression, but I read the lines of his body as he leaned against the door frame. Just waiting. His stillness poured through my body like steamy coffee on a winter day. That's why I was here: he was different.

It wasn't that Colin was never pushy or controlling, because he excelled at both those skills. The difference was that, whatever he did, he wouldn't harm me. Not ever. I couldn't even make him do it. I should know—I had tried. It was as if I'd been searching for him without even knowing it, trying out random men at a bar in the world's stupidest litmus test.

And now that I'd found him, the trick was how not to lose him. I got out of the car and strode up the sidewalk. He stepped aside and, with a nod of his head, invited me in. As I passed, I could feel the tension vibrating within him—curiosity, frustration, maybe lust—carefully caged within thick walls of patience.

He took my coat. I followed the trail of savory aromas to the kitchen and set the dessert I'd brought on the counter.

"Drink?" he asked.

"Sure. That would be... Thanks."

"Wine? Beer?"

"Oh." I didn't usually drink alcohol except for my club nights. The numbing effects would be welcomed now, except I needed to keep it together tonight. Didn't want to go spilling secrets, after all. "Maybe just water."

He handed me a glass. "We've got a few minutes before the pot roast is done."

"Mmm, pot roast." It had been forever since I'd had real meat, not the rubbery stuff that came in canned soup. Since my last date with Colin, actually. "It smells amazing."

"It's from the restaurant." He quirked his lips. "With scalloped potatoes."

I grinned. "So you're a meat and potatoes kind of guy."

He shrugged. "I'm pretty simple."

I snorted. Simple as a Rubik's Cube. But all I said was, "Maybe."

The white cabinets, Formica countertops, and tiled backsplash matched the quaintness of the house but looked new. The stainless-steel appliances and fixtures completed the picture of a modern kitchen. But I'd expect nothing less from the owner of a restaurant. I might have been envious if I had ever imagined such things for myself.

I peered back the way we'd come, through the dining room.

"Did you want me to show you around?" he asked.

"Yes." I smiled. I noted his hesitation and his stiffness, but I did want to see his house. Every little detail, from the green splash of color from the tea towel to the prickly aloe plant that sat on the counter, was a piece of Colin. I would hoard that knowledge like a miser collects coins and later strums through them with his fingers just for the pleasure of it.

Despite the coziness of the house, there was a definite sparseness to its furnishing. So male. So Colin. Plush seating and dark wood furniture stood so perfectly in place, without clutter, that I half expected to see price tags hanging on them.

Colin was quiet, even for him. And watchful. He walked ahead of me, leading me to the different rooms—the living room, the dining room, a study. And outside, the back porch overlooking a small but lush lawn. I oohed and ahhed. It came naturally, this admiration, because his house was beautiful and stark, like him. The place was large enough to be roomy, but small enough to be cozy. It was, as Goldilocks would say in Bailey's book, just right. But I felt like he was waiting for something specific in my responses.

I leaned my elbows on the wood rail of the back patio as if I belonged. "It's a great house."

"Do you think so?" he asked. It didn't sound like the idle question it should have been.

"Absolutely. It's perfect. Why? You aren't thinking of selling it, are you?"

"If I did, would you buy it?"

I laughed. "There's no way I could afford this house. How much does something like this run? One hundred thousand?"

A faint blush tinted his cheeks, and I knew it had cost more. Not that I could even afford a fraction of that. It might as well have been a castle for all that it was accessible to me.

"The food's probably ready," he said, and we went back inside the house.

I found the dishes while he transferred the food from metal pots to ceramic platters. We met at the dining table amid clanking utensils. I set a place for him at the head of the table and sat next to him. That left five empty chairs and a wide expanse of cherry wood table.

"Do you have company often?" I asked.

His eyes flicked over the table, all those empty chairs. "No."

I took a bite of the pot roast. The juices exploded in my mouth, and I released a soft moan. "God, this is good."

A quick smile. "I'm glad you like it."

"I bet you get that all the time."

He shrugged. "It's nice to eat a meal here, for once. And to have company." My face heated. "How's Bailey?"

I blinked. "She's fine. And your brother?"

"Also fine."

Have you talked to him lately? I wanted to ask. *Done anything illegal? Dangerous?* But his eyes warned me away. I wouldn't like the answer.

We moved on to safer topics. My work at the bakery and his at his restaurant. We both worked with food—something so elemental, providing sustenance, health. In my case, not so much health, but there's a special intimacy that comes from preparing food for someone, as he had cooked this dinner and I had baked that pie.

We ate and were merry, as merry as Colin ever was. It was a last meal, of sorts. When we'd both eaten too much, Colin took me to the living room.

His hand caught mine, tender, and his eyes captured mine, intent. "What's wrong?"

"Nothing," I said in a falsetto.

"Tell me," he said.

I sighed. The man was a walking lie detector. Either that or I was transparent as fuck. "Something happened," I said. "Bailey…well, her father has come back."

His face showed no reaction.

I averted my eyes before continuing. An omission was still a lie. "He was a friend of mine. From school. And we…hooked up. And then he left town. Now he's back, and he wants to see Bailey. At least that's what he said, but I don't trust him. He doesn't care about her. He's just using her to get to me."

Those dark brown eyes revealed nothing. "What are you going to do?"

"I don't really know what I *can* do. I guess visitation

is something that would have to be figured out in court. But I would… *strongly prefer*… that he not get to see us at all."

Colin's eyes sharpened. "What's wrong with him?"

I blinked away the answering thoughts. "Nothing. I mean, it's not like he's ready to be a father. He just wants to mess with me, but he…he had a rough childhood. I mean, really bad."

"He ever hit you?" His voice was soft, but even if I couldn't have sensed the banked fury within him, I knew from experience what he could do to a man who hurt me. Even if I could've gotten the words out, I couldn't tell him, not without risking Colin going after Andrew, hurting them both.

I was grateful that the phrasing of the question allowed my "no" to be the truth. He hadn't hit me, not exactly. But I knew I had to be more specific if I wanted Colin's help. "He's just not completely…stable. He drinks too much, and he uses. He picks up and leaves whenever he wants. And when he's angry…well, I don't want Bailey around him."

"You need money," he said.

"Sort of. I have money…" Not enough, probably, but that wasn't what I wanted. I wanted safety. And him. "I mean, I'm not sure how much it'll be, but—"

"I'm not rich, but I have enough for this." He looked like a man calculating the odds. Unnecessary, really, since I was woefully out of my league. This wasn't a negotiation as much as total surrender. "I'll help you."

I gave Colin a look.

He raised his eyebrows, all innocence. "I meant the right way. I can find a decent lawyer. We'll fight him, legally. In the meantime, move in with me."

"What?" Hadn't seen that one coming. "That's...that's insane."

He actually rolled his eyes, making him look more like the twentysomething that he was. "People move in together all the time."

"Not after dating for a week," I said.

"I'm counting since the first time."

"In case you forgot," I said, "I have a baby. A kid."

"I didn't forget. There's room for her. Besides, your apartment is a shithole."

Harsh. Even worse, he was right. "You're completely frustrating."

He raised one eyebrow, which somehow proved my words irrelevant in one smooth swoop.

I set down my fork, taking his offer seriously. "We barely know each other."

"We know each other enough," he said. "From the first it was different."

It was only the truth. Ever since my sordid proposition at the bar, there had been something between us. A spark, or maybe just recognition that he could handle my brand of crazy. I'd tried to ignore it and had even gone back to the bar to disprove it, but nothing had worked. What was this thing that felt like trust but looked like lust?

"But why?" I said, desperate to deny him or find some excuse to accept. "Just tell me why you'd even want that?"

"I have reasons."

"But you aren't going to tell them to me."

"It's okay, what happened before." He pulled me close. "You're with me now."

The words were pitched perfectly, but they bounced off the wall of secrets I kept between us. I'd left out the most important part. What would he do if he found out?

I shivered, and he encircled me in his arms. Keeping me, for now.

"Can you spend the night?" he asked.

"Yes." I had already put Bailey to sleep in Shelly's bed. This was the third time in as many weeks, but Shelly graciously claimed not to mind about the loss of income.

"Good," he murmured.

He took me to his bedroom upstairs. It was just as plain as all the other rooms, just as casual. Home, but I couldn't think about that. Instead I tried to psych myself up. Please him, pay my dues, when all I really wanted to do was have sex with him. I wanted to rip off my clothes and his. In my wildest thoughts I wanted to push his face down between my legs and tell him to do that thing again.

Instead I just stood there in his bedroom like I'd never been inside a man's bedroom before. Which was almost true, except for Andrew's.

He turned down the sheets. When he glanced back, his eyes softened. "Come here."

I averted my eyes while he tugged my dress over my head. He gestured to the bed, and I kicked off my shoes and climbed in, still in my underwear and bra. After stripping down to his boxers, he followed me in.

I wished I didn't feel this strange nervousness. It felt almost like a wedding night. How awful.

Colin turned me away from him. I expected him to take off my bra or fuck me from behind, but he was working from a totally different playbook, because what he did was pull me in close to his body and *cuddle.* Christ, we were spooning. And not as a sexual position. Although there was a certain hardness pressing into my ass, it was doing absolutely no nudging, no rocking, and no thrusting. Whoever heard of a hard, docile cock?

Ah, hell. We'd skipped the wedding night and gone straight to married.

Well.

I pushed my ass back slightly, gratified by the catch in his breath. His arm tightened around my waist, but his hips remained still. Another nudge of my ass, this time triggering a twitch of that hardness.

Yes, that's it. I rocked back into him. He had wanted me, the slut. And sluts were for sex. No more thinking, no more feeling. No more worry. At least for tonight, I got to play the slut and still be safe.

When I felt his hand drift around to my hips, my lips curved into a smile. *Gotcha.* Then his hands skimmed over my stomach and beneath my panties, and my smile slipped and my eyelids lowered.

Rough fingers prodded me open. One finger worked inside me, a little deeper each time my hips rocked into his hand. And thank God—finally!—his hips pushed against mine. At the knowledge that he was into this, a participant, my mind slipped a little closer into that blissful space of submission. But God, I wanted so much more. He was capable of more.

"What's wrong?" I whispered.

"You want this, don't you?" He repeated his words from earlier, still worrying over my consent. No, nothing like the others. Tears sprung into my eyes, and I was grateful he couldn't see them.

"I want this. I want you." I could only hope he took the thickness of my voice for arousal. "I want you to give it to me hard. Be rough, Colin. Do it." Even before I'd finished speaking, his fingers inside me and his cock rubbing against my ass sped up, roughened.

His other arm slipped under me, holding me flush against him. As if I was going anywhere. But I was totally cocooned now, at his mercy. His fingers hit a certain spot inside me, and a soft cry escaped me. My hips jerked in a frantic rhythm, reaching for it, begging.

But it wasn't his fingers rubbing me that took me over. It was the sharp pant of his breath on my neck. His excitement, mine. And as my climax took me, I shook in his arms, falling apart, held together.

As I collapsed into his hardness, my heart felt over-full. Desperate to turn this into something familiar, something sexual, I grabbed his wrist and sucked his wet fingers.

I swirled my tongue around his fingers like a cock, offering.

He shifted on the bed so that he lay flat, accepting.

I crawled—prowled, really—on my hands and knees between his legs. The tense arousal on his face made me feel sensual, powerful. There *was* a certain power to my role, that I could incite this man to lust. He pulled down his boxers, and, with his hands in my hair, slipped my mouth over his cock. That'd been the shortest power trip ever.

Down and up, he directed me. Steadily, inexorably forcing more of his smooth, hard skin into me. My focus narrowed to my senses, what I could see or taste or feel. Every time I lost my way, he brought me back with his fingers at my neck, a soft grunt or a tensing of his thighs beneath my hands.

It wasn't about sucking cock. This was Colin guiding, and me yielding. Colin giving, and me receiving. Or was it the other way around? It didn't matter, so long as it never ended. There was a certain urgency about him, more than a man wanting to come, and I answered it by taking him deeper.

Even as my jaw tired and my eyes watered, I felt his pleasure like it was my own. His labored breathing, his fingers tightening in my hair, the small thrust of his hips—I wanted it all. My fingers fumbled, wrapping around him, stroking him below, fondling delicate skin.

Suddenly he surged up. Next thing I knew I was on my back, knees bent, and Colin deep inside me.

I gasped, belated.

"Fuck," he said.

He wrenched back, then fished a condom out of the nightstand. A few seconds respite and then he thrust back inside me. He was too deep to move. Too deep to breathe.

"Colin." Pleas had never worked, but he stilled.

With his nostrils flaring and a light sheen of sweat on his face, Colin looked savage. "Hurt you?"

"No, I…"

He rocked against me slightly, straining. "You what?"

I want you. Don't leave me. "Fuck me."

He did.

And then I feel asleep, enfolded in thick arms, feeling like Alice falling down the rabbit hole.

CHAPTER TWELVE

SUNLIGHT BEAMED DIRECTLY into my closed eyes, but how? Cheap vinyl blinds provided little relief, but my window backed up directly to the next apartment building. Besides which, it was coated in decades of goop.

My nose tickled. I took a deep breath and smelled—a man. Shit.

I snapped my eyes open. Chest hair. A familiar face. Ah, Colin. Safe. I shut my eyes again, fully intending to employ a fake-it-till-you-make-it approach to sleep.

The brightness pricked behind my eyelids. I peeked one eye open and glared at the big bay window with no curtains. This house needed a woman's touch.

The night rushed back to me like the pop of a balloon. Well, damn. Looked like that was my job now.

Speaking of which, a certain piece of hot, hard flesh pressed into my hip.

Last night was the first time I hadn't showered shortly after sex. I always had done so immediately after my date nights, even with Colin. Despite the fact that he'd used a condom, I felt surprisingly sticky—everywhere. I supposed it should be hot, the remains of sex, the morning after, but it was…awkward.

Naked, I slipped from Colin's unconscious grip.

The bathroom held only the basics: a bar of soap, a bottle of shampoo-conditioner, shaving supplies. The shiny surfaces shone, too clean for a bachelor's place. Had he just moved in? That would explain the minimalist but catalog-perfect furniture and lack of decor. I made a mental note to ask him and decided he wouldn't mind if I took a shower.

I stood under the spray and flipped the tap all the way to hot, relishing the biting cold that steeped into a blissful scald. As I lathered myself using the minty bar of soap, I heard a snick from the door and Colin's voice. "Excuse me." Excuse what? I peered around the shower curtain to see two pale, *tight* ass cheeks, then snatched the curtain back in place with a squeak.

Damn.

He was using the potty. No, the toilet. Fuck! I was an adult. It was called a toilet.

"You okay?" He sounded amused.

"I'm fine." I clutched the soap, which slipped from my hands onto the tub with a thud.

"Sure?"

I picked up the soap. "Never better."

"Can you move today?"

I dropped the soap again. "Fuck!"

"What?"

"Nothing. Ahhh, moving. Hmm…" To be honest I hadn't been entirely sure we were doing that, or whether the whole thing had been some weird date dream. And I really hadn't expected it so soon, but leave it to Colin to be expedient.

"I don't know," I said. "Can we talk about it later? I have to go in to work this afternoon."

"About that," he said.

I didn't like his tone. I poked my head out of the shower. Colin leaned against the bathroom counter, somehow looking not at all silly while totally naked—and hard.

"I was thinking you could quit," he said.

I gaped but managed to eke out a, "What?"

He shrugged in the face of my shock. "It sucks. The pay is shit, and so are the hours. You don't even like it."

He added that as an afterthought, but of course, I *didn't* like it. Damn him for knowing that. "Wait a minute. How do you know how much I make?"

His eyes flickered. "You work shifts in a low-end bakery. How much can it pay? Besides, I'm in the industry."

That made sense, I supposed. But still… "It would take time to find a better job. How would I pay my share?"

"I didn't ask you to move in because I need a roommate, Allie."

The effect of his sarcasm was offset by the teasing light in his eyes. I tightened my grip on the shower curtain to shield myself from the cold air and his hotness. "How will I pay you back for the lawyer?"

He snorted. "It wasn't going to be a loan. Besides…there won't really be a regular bill."

That alarmed me.

"Relax," he said. "He's a real lawyer. He's already on retainer, that's all, with my brother."

I wanted nothing to do with his brother, and Colin knew it. I especially didn't like the idea of using his lawyer, someone who might have a different agenda. And worse, if the lawyer was paid by Colin's brother, I'd owe *him*.

"No," I said.

Colin didn't look the least bit perturbed, as if he'd known I'd say that.

"It's not about the money. He's good at what he does." Colin paused to give me a look, confirming that yes, the guy had gotten them out of illegal shit before. "I wouldn't trust just any lawyer to help with this, seeing as, well…fathers have legal rights. Visitation, joint custody." He shrugged away the awful words.

"I see," I said through clenched teeth. "If you think he deserves visitation and…custody, why are you helping me?"

Colin looked me straight in the eyes. "I don't think he deserves anything. I don't give a fuck about him. I'm doing this because you want it, and I'm going to get it for you." Then he turned and walked out of the bathroom.

My heart beat against my chest, hard and fierce.

It was a rather dark shade of gray, his declaration, but

I didn't think I'd ever heard anything more romantic than Colin telling me he'd spend his money, break laws, do anything he had to, to give me what I wanted. He was the man I'd been looking for without even trying. The man I hadn't believed existed, one who'd fight for me. One who'd win.

CHAPTER THIRTEEN

MY BEST FRIEND in fifth grade was my neighbor two doors down, Leslie Pritchard. We didn't like each other all that much, but absentee parenting made for strange bedfellows.

Leslie was lonely on nights her mom worked, and so she got a kitten. Leslie and I would sit around in the evenings playing with him, and as if the kitten were our campfire, he would jump in the air and flick his frizzy orange tail.

She'd toss a string, and he would leap with abandon only to come crashing down to the thin carpet in a tumble of tiny limbs. Bug—that was his name—didn't know that cats should always land on their feet, and he remained staunchly flippant throughout his adolescent years up until he got run over by my dad's truck. That day marked the end of my friendship with Leslie Pritchard.

The cats around my old apartment were nothing like Bug. They scattered as I climbed the steps, Bailey in one hand, a double-layer cake in the other. All I needed was a handless trombone and I could star in a Dr. Seuss book.

I slid Bailey down my leg so I could knock.

My gaze traced the lines of peeling paint on the door, maroon with white underneath and a trace of blue between them. Like the rings in a tree, marking the time. It had been two days since I'd fled Colin's house, making empty promises about *calling him* and *soon*. I knew what I had to do, but it could be hard to leave home, even if home was a shitty apartment in the scary side of town.

Shelly opened the door.

"Hey, ladies." Her voice was hoarse, and her smile didn't quite reach her bloodshot eyes.

Shit, shit, shit. Maybe it was just the tiredness resulting from staying up late. But this was Tuesday, and she usually didn't have a client on Monday. In fact, I left her alone most of the time on Mondays to let her sleep it off. Besides, lack of sleep wasn't enough to affect her like this. Shelly was like a prey animal. Her problems never manifested in her appearance. If she looked like this, then things had truly gone to shit.

"Shelly?"

Her eyes slid away. She opened her mouth, to answer maybe, but then clapped a hand over it. Leaving the door open for us, she stumbled back through the hallway. The thud of the bathroom door punctuated her departure.

I found Shelly curled up on her bed on top of the covers. Bailey tried to go to her, but I distracted her with a chunk of cake that would be hell to clean up later.

I returned to the bedside. "Jesus, Shelly. Which one?"

"Things just got out of hand," she mumbled, her eyes closed.

It had been a stupid question, because the answer didn't matter. She could hardly go to the police. I'd been too afraid to ask the important question, but I asked it now. "How bad is it?"

"Not bad."

I sighed. "Just tell me. I'm going to find out anyway."

She looked so thin. When she swaggered around, dressed provocatively and with that half smile, she looked every inch the femme fatale. But lying there, she seemed almost childlike. I reached for her, my hand hovering in the air as if she might break if I touched her. Except she'd already been broken. I gingerly pulled up her shirt to reveal angry, red welts that streaked the length of her back and down under her jeans. I'd seen them before, back when Shelly had first started in the life, before she had regulars to keep her safe.

"He did this," I said, my voice detached from my head as if I had a cold. I meant the one who liked to rough her up. I told her not to see him, and usually she didn't take on clients like him, but there was something about him that kept her going back.

"It wasn't him. I took on a new client."

"Why? Why would you do that?"

She gestured toward the nightstand, and I opened the drawer. On top of the mess of beauty products and a few books was a single white envelope. A thick one.

I looked inside. Money, and lots of it.

"Shit," came out on my exhale.

"Five thousand." Pride colored her voice—I didn't

know whether that was a good sign or bad. Five thousand fucking dollars. That was ten times her regular nightly rate, as much money as she made in a month. Of course, she wouldn't be able to work now for the next couple of weeks, with her back all torn up.

"But why? We agreed you wouldn't do shit like this. Christ, Shelly. You could have been really hurt. You *are* really hurt."

"It's for the lawyer," she said. "A retainer or some shit."

Oh, fuck. No.

I threw the envelope into the open drawer, hundred dollar bills spilling out in a vulgar array.

"We need a lawyer. You know that. You can't run from this. Where would you go? A lawyer will figure this out. Make it right."

I couldn't even think about that, not in the face of her gory sacrifice. "You did not do that for me. Tell me you didn't do that."

She sighed like I was the irresponsible one. I wanted to rail at her, except she'd already been beaten, hadn't she? And for me.

I thought I'd known what my own stupidity would cost the people I loved, but I'd been wrong. My father had been doubtful of my future, but I'd cinched the deal when I'd ended up pregnant and alone. Parenting was a laughable term for the desperation with which I kept Bailey in generic-brand baby food.

I'd even failed Andrew. No one understood, not even Shelly. He had lusted after me, wanted me, all that time, not that I'd deserved such devotion. I should have walked away from our friendship once I found out. Or maybe just sucked it up and been with him. Anything other than remain friends but without fucking him. That was my mistake.

And that night. I'd done a million things wrong that night. I shouldn't have worn that dress or hung out with him alone or stayed there with him when he'd been drinking. But most of all I shouldn't have said no, because then it would have just been sex. It would have been a hookup, not rape. And right now I wouldn't be a victim.

I'd allowed Shelly to be an escort—no, a prostitute—all this time. Not that it was my prerogative strictly, but I could've made her stop. I should have found a way to make her stop.

Bailey fussed, mashing the last bit of frosting into the carpet, but I stood rooted to the spot, my eyes stinging.

"Hey," Shelly said softly. "You didn't ask me to do it. Don't take that on yourself. I want this fixed as much as you do, okay? It was for me. You have to take it."

I took the money. I had to, because she'd given up strips of her skin for it, and the very least I could do was make it worth something.

With dry eyes I washed Bailey up and brought her into the room. In that age-old way of children she seemed to recognize Shelly was hurt. She curled up in Shelly's arms and planted a sloppy, wet kiss on her cheek. I circled the bed and crawled in from the other side.

I wanted to hold Shelly, to be the big spoon, but she

wouldn't appreciate being touched like that, especially not now with her back torn up. So I settled for facing her back on my side, like a sentry, until she settled into sleep.

Some preternatural sense told me to stay. Not to protect her from the men who hit her—as if I could—but instead from the monsters that haunted her. Or maybe just to protect her from herself.

Downstairs seemed too far, too risky, when her hand clutched the pillow so tightly. So I tucked Bailey into the bed right in the middle and watched over them. There was a peace in the dark, in the quiet, where even my thoughts could still.

I didn't want to be like the alley cats, terrified of everything. They'd rather live wretchedly than take a chance. A leap of faith. I had spent a lot of time fighting men—and fighting myself. I'd managed to hurt myself over and over again, all to prove I didn't need to trust a man.

Except I did trust a man. *Colin.*

It came from deep inside, that trust, unexpected and even unwanted. He slipped under my defenses with his quiet solidity. If a man had tried to persuade me, to cajole me into moving in with him, I never could have. It was only his bluntness, his cold and steady regard that could have swayed me.

He said he'd protect me, and for some reason I believed him.

He could protect Bailey, and she deserved that.

I slipped from the bed and called Colin. Then I tucked myself back in beside Bailey and went to sleep.

Chapter Fourteen

THE ONLY FANFARE for my grand dive into trust was a soft knock on Shelly's door. I opened it and gave him a half smile, uncertain how to treat him.

"Hey," I said softly.

"Hello," he said, and I was struck by the formality until Shelly answered from behind me.

"Colin—nice to meet you," she said.

Bailey burbled a greeting.

"I brought boxes," Colin said, nodding to the parking lot.

"Boxes?" Shelly asked with a lilt of accusation.

"Yes, well." I cleared my throat. "Colin asked me to move in with him, and…I agreed."

I held my breath. If she hated me, if I'd hurt her, I'd never forgive myself.

Shelly smiled. Not the perfect, blinding, fake one she got paid for, but a real, lopsided grin that made her a million times prettier. "That's great."

I smiled back, relieved. "You're not upset?"

She patted my hand. "About time we got out of this rat's nest."

Of course. She only lived in this dump because it was

all I could afford. She deserved better, and that alone was enough to convince me that I was making the right choice. It felt like giving up control—my apartment, my job, my fight with Andrew—but I'd been treading water on my own for too long. If I could make this better for Bailey, for Shelly, then it was worth the risk.

"Now go on," she said. "You pack. I'll watch Bailey."

Relieved, I gave her a peck on the cheek, which she accepted with the forbearance of a queen. I practically skipped down the steps with Colin at my heels. We each grabbed a handful of flattened boxes from the back of his truck before going to my apartment door.

As I put the key to the lock, the door swung open an inch. The lock itself cocked, exposing the circular hole it occupied in the door. I stood there blankly until Colin shook me.

"Go upstairs," he said. "Now."

It registered then—my apartment had been broken into. I ran upstairs and back into Shelly's place, where I snatched Bailey up. She was safe. She squirmed, but I held her even tighter. Shelly questioned me, and I must have said something. What if Bailey had been there?

Shelly opened the door to Colin.

"They're gone," he said.

"Who could have…?" Shelly trailed off. It was better unfinished.

"Pack quickly," Colin said.

I went cautiously back downstairs, as if I were going to survey the aftermath of a hurricane. But there was no disaster, not outwardly. Nothing had been taken—not that I had anything valuable—and nothing had been destroyed. Just the lock on the door, broken by some faceless person.

A violation. I should be used to them by now.

It was probably just a prank. Or a robbery that ended in disappointment when all they found were dolls and toys.

This place was crappy, but it had been home—mine. It shouldn't matter because we were going to a place that was so much better—Colin's. I tried to focus my thoughts on the practical, like throwing clothes into trash bags.

Colin loaded the crib and high chair and other furniture into his truck. That meant leaving behind my bed, my dishes, my dinette. Colin said he would come back later and take whatever was left to Goodwill. We filled up his truck and my car trunk, and I realized just how few material possessions I had.

Shelly brought Bailey down when we were finished.

She paused for another hug as she handed Bailey over. I glanced at Colin. He was strapping down the stuff in his truck.

"The lock—" I started.

"Don't think about it," she said.

She was right of course, but… "Am I making a mistake?"

"Of course not." Her face was perfectly smooth, gaze clear, completely giving herself away, the faker.

"You're a horrible liar."

She raised two perfectly groomed eyebrows. "I have a buttload of clients who say otherwise."

"Yeah, well, I know you too well." I lowered my voice. "I'm scared."

"What's the worst that could happen?" she said.

We both laughed. She always knew how to cheer me up.

Because, well, the worst was pretty bad, but then we'd both been through bad. What Shelly meant was that bad things happen, but we couldn't let them rule us. Living was a choice.

Colin slammed the tailgate shut and turned to me.

He raised his eyebrow. *You still in?*

Yes, I answered silently.

BAILEY DUG THROUGH my box of clothes while I hung them up in the closet. The room had two closets, so this one had been empty when we got here. Still, it was already stocked with hangers, and that had to count for something.

Colin stepped in. "I've got the last of it downstairs."

"Thanks." I wiped my palms on my jeans.

Christ, how awkward. Why had no one ever given me lessons on how to handle moving in with a guy I barely knew? Suddenly that seemed like a vital life skill.

"So." I took one of my high heels out of Bailey's hands and replaced it with an innocuous sweater. "It's official."

"Yeah." He had an almost cautious expression, as if I was freaking out.

Was I freaking out? Possibly a little. "We're cool, right?"

Humor glinted in his eyes, turning them from glacial to just chilly. "We're good. But listen, I've got to head out."

Alarm streaked through me. "You're leaving?"

He frowned, just a crease of his forehead, but I didn't think it was directed at me. "It just came up." He shook his head as if to negate the importance. "I'll be back by dinner."

"Right, okay."

He gave me a speculative look. I strove for casual and failed. With a grimace I took as an attempted smile, he left the room. A few minutes later I heard his truck bump out of the driveway.

"Bye-bye," Bailey said.

"That's right!" I winced as my feigned cheerfulness came out louder than anticipated. "He's gone bye-bye. But he'll be back soon, promise!"

Back by dinner, apparently. Should I make dinner? I made dinner for Bailey and myself every day, of course, but I wouldn't feel right serving Colin spaghetti from a can. He probably thought I could cook, seeing as I baked, but it wasn't the same. Give me flour and sugar over turmeric any day.

I quickly finished up with the clothes; then Bailey

and I forged into the kitchen. I expected a barren refrigerator, save for lumpy milk and beer. There'd be stale chips in the cupboard for sure. Instead what I found was a chef's paradise. A fully stocked fridge with vegetables. A pantry with buckets of grains I couldn't even name.

He *did* own a restaurant. I was so fucked.

But I didn't have a choice. Most likely he did expect dinner, and besides, it seemed fair and right. Even with my income from the bakery, I couldn't cover a fraction of the costs of this place. Of course I should contribute this way.

I rummaged through the fridge, past fancy cheeses and free-range eggs and vegetables that just reeked of organic, when I heard the crash behind me. Bailey had helped herself to the pantry, her chubby arm jammed in a box of whole wheat graham crackers. She fished out a still-wrapped plastic package and held it up triumphantly.

"Crackers," she said with a baby chuckle.

"Glad one of us is already at home."

She fussed at the plastic until I pulled it open for her. That pantry would need reorganization—namely, the entire bottom shelf should be empty—but that would wait for another day.

I foraged for something easy, like pasta, and came up empty until I found the lasagna slices. Sure enough, there was marinara among the sauces, ricotta among the cheeses, and grass-fed ground beef in the freezer. Hell,

I'd eaten lasagna before. Mostly frozen, but it was self-explanatory, what with those layers.

I even got fancy, sautéing onions and chopping parsley, while Bailey built a sand castle on the once-gleaming kitchen floor. I did a double take. Yes, she had crumbled what was probably an entire box of graham crackers into some sort of sandlike state. She sat in the middle, gleefully trailing her grubby fingers through the layer like it was her personal zen garden.

"Oh, Bailey," I groaned.

She sucked on her crumb-coated fingers, but I couldn't even be upset about the mess when the state of the entire kitchen smacked me like a frying pan. It was a disaster. The counters were piled with food in varying states of cooked.

I laid the layers of lasagna and stuck it in the oven, then set about cleaning. First I put away all the produce and ingredients. Then I grabbed the pan to wash it and burned my hand in the process.

Ouch. Leave it to some fancy brand of cookware to actually have fewer features than a cheapo knockoff, like say, plastic handles for safety. Probably they were expecting rich people not to be idiots and spring for pot holders. Fair enough.

Bailey watched me curiously as I ran my hand under the cold water, and I realized I'd been making monkey-like sounds in my pain.

A smile slid across my face. "Mommy silly?"

In response she puffed up proudly and presented her

hand, covered in crumbs. "Cracker!"

My shoulders slumped. "Right."

Although I had plenty left to do cleaning my own mess, I figured I'd fix the floor first. For all I knew, he'd take one look at the nuclear wasteland that was his kitchen and order us out into the street. Okay, probably not that drastic, but it wouldn't be good.

He wasn't used to living with a kid. Even if he was, graham cracker snowfall was not an everyday occurrence. So I cleaned like a woman possessed. I would not even mention that regular graham crackers did not crumble on touching them. It was probably the grains, being whole as they were, but he wouldn't hear that from me.

Possibly I was becoming unhinged. A hysterical laugh bubbled up, but I ruthlessly forced it down. I was going to make this work. Everything was going to be fine, and if it wasn't...well. Well.

I swept up the crumbs, though the wet ones got caught in the broom's bristles and had to be washed out. Then I went back over the floor with paper towels, but the particles had wormed their way into the grout, as if it could camouflage itself with cement. I scrubbed until my hand was tired, but this called for stronger stuff.

I ducked my head into the cabinet under the sink, rummaging for some harsh chemical shit to wipe those suckers out.

"Uh, Allie?"

In a knee-jerk reaction, I banged my head into the wood above me. A cry escaped me as tears sprang to my eyes. A sense of utter failure assailed me, and I contemplated just how long I could keep my head buried in the cupboard before it got weird. Not very long, it turned out, because Colin dragged me off the floor and into a kitchen chair with such horribly insensitive commentary as "Jesus" and "Are you okay?"

"I made a mess," I said flatly.

In acknowledgment he gently pressed an ice pack to my head.

I flinched, then let him hold me steady. "I'm sorry."

"Hey." That was all he said, his chiding tone tempered with concern.

The tears fell in streams then, making my voice all high and wavery as I tried to explain. "I'm sorry. I know you said dinner, and I tried to make it, but I just didn't… I didn't have *time*, you know? Or the ability to cook, either. I'm so sorry."

"Stop apologizing," he cut in.

"But—"

"No, listen. I didn't mean you'd have to cook. I can cook, or we can go out. Don't stress out."

"I am so beyond stressed," I said, watery.

"Let's order a pizza."

The consideration and utter simplicity of the gesture touched me. "Really?"

He handed the ice pack off to me and pulled out his cell phone. "Ordering now. What do you want?"

"But the organic," I said. "And the grass feeding. I know you don't just order pizza."

"Pepperoni with extra chemicals? Got it," he said to me before he turned to the phone to place a real order.

I swiped at the tears, but they didn't want to stop. While relief flooded me, I toyed with the empty box of lasagna noodles on the kitchen table. Idly I read the fine print.

"Hell," I said. "You're supposed to boil these first?"

"Silly mommy," Bailey said.

CHAPTER FIFTEEN

IF I THOUGHT I'd made a mess in Colin's kitchen, it was nothing compared to the bakery.

Cabinet doors were open, pans littered the countertops, and a fine layer of flour coated the entire room. It hadn't even been this messy that time a hailstorm had knocked in the front windows.

I stepped inside, my mouth open. No one was in the back. The restroom was dark. I peeked into the storefront. Empty.

That left Rick's office. The door was shut, and I was almost afraid to knock. The place looked like a crime scene. First-degree baking by an idiot, maybe. I couldn't muster up the proper seriousness when the place looked like a supersized snow globe.

A deep breath. Knowing Rick, this was going to get strange. Well, stranger than usual.

I knocked. "Rick?"

Scuffling sounds from within. Then Rick poked his head out the door. "Allie. What are you doing here?"

"It's my shift. What happened?"

"What happened?" he repeated.

I closed my eyes tight, prayed for patience, then

opened them. "Here. In the kitchen. It's like a flour bomb went off."

"Oh, right." He glanced past me as if just noticing the mess.

I narrowed my eyes. "Seriously, what happened?"

"Nothing. No work today. Bakery's closed. Go home." And he shut the door in my face.

Oh man, I would love nothing better than to go home, to pick up Bailey from Shelly's and maybe even convince Shelly to spend the afternoon out with us. But even as I planned my afternoon off, I stomped my foot. A cloud of flour rose up, and I sneezed. I couldn't leave. Rick was a friend. An annoying, clearly deranged friend, but there was no way I could walk away from this. Whatever this was.

I knocked again, harder. "Rick!"

A thud and then a curse. He opened the door. "Why did you yell?"

"Let me in."

A pause. "No."

"Then come out here."

"Definitely no."

"You have exactly three seconds to open this door, or I swear to God I will..."

Before I had to make up a false threat, he opened the door. Files and papers flooded the small office. The cheap wood furniture peeked out between crumpled pages. I shouldn't have even been surprised.

Rick turned away and squatted to rifle through a

bookcase. Rather halfheartedly, considering the magnitude of disarray.

"What the hell, Rick? Now."

He stopped and bowed his head. Then he turned and stood, with so much raw emotion on his face that my breath caught. In the year and a half that I'd worked here, I'd never figured him out, but in this moment his eyes told the whole story.

Nothing so mundane as details. The broken, raw, painful part of me recognized the same thing in him. We stood there, connected by this nothing, and everything. It was uncomfortably intimate. More intimate than sex, but I'd learned long ago that the recognition of pain was so much more potent than the sharing of pleasure.

He leaned in, his intent clear. I didn't want to kiss him. He was a friend to me. Maybe even a surrogate father, since mine never came around. And there was Colin.

I jerked back, just slightly.

He froze, and then smiled a small, sad good-bye. It was a relief, to see he understood and accepted it, and a confirmation that we'd been real friends. A small rush of air escaped me. It was a miserable thing, not knowing a friend from an enemy.

"Allie," he whispered. "Come with me."

"Where are you going?"

"Away. Let's leave this place. I've got a little money saved up. It'll be just us."

Even if there wasn't Colin or Shelly, I wouldn't have.

Probably not. But stupidly, the first thing that popped into my head was, "What about Bailey?"

"She'll come, too, of course."

I shook my head against the crazy. "What are you saying? We aren't going anywhere. You have the bakery. And I have…well, I have roots here." That was an exaggeration. I had history here, in this city, which wasn't quite the same. And I had Shelly, who'd just as soon transplant with me.

Colin counted as roots, however young and tender they may be.

I had to see him again. Right now.

Rick was searching again, picking through the papers like they were rubble from an explosion and babbling about finding things and running out of time. I wanted to help him, but sometimes I had to learn when to walk away. When I wasn't really wanted or needed. And Rick, for all that he cared about me in his own way and had asked me to go away with him, was in his own world. I was a prop, not a player.

I put a hand on Rick's arm, and he stopped moving. He looked up at me, lost.

"I'm going to go now. I've moved in with someone."

"Okay," he said. "I'm sorry."

"You have nothing to be sorry for," I told him. "But…I quit."

The relief on his face was answered by gratitude within me. There weren't words, so I pressed a soft kiss to his lips before leaving the bakery for the last time.

CHAPTER SIXTEEN

"IS LIVING WITH a man all it's cracked up to be?" Shelly asked as she examined her nails.

I studied her, unsure if she was being sarcastic or not. A mist of caution had risen between us in the few days I'd been at Colin's. "Oh, you know. The toilet seat's up, and there's extra laundry. That's about it."

She glanced up, a small curve to her lips. "You do his laundry?"

My lips answered hers in a smile. "Yeah."

"Isn't it sort of…weird? I mean, *underwear*." She lowered her voice—this from the girl who'd taught me everything I knew about how to give great head.

I ducked behind my pizza slice as I took a bite. It *was* weird. Blowing a guy was one thing, folding his underwear seemed so…personal.

Still, I'd insisted. I picked up all the housework and even got a cookbook. It was the least I could do, considering I wasn't contributing financially.

Speaking of which. "Where've you been staying? I stopped by the other day."

Shelly grabbed another slice from the box and began picking off the toppings. She always picked everything off, though she insisted on ordering supreme. It added variety, she always said. "At a friend's place."

"A friend?" I didn't mean to sound so skeptical, but she and I weren't exactly the book club type. It had just been me and her. At least since Andrew had…well, since Andrew.

"A client," she said.

That was new. Brand, spanking, completely against the rules new. I opened my mouth—to warn her, to chastise her—but she was a big girl, and I wasn't quite that much of a hypocrite. In fact, that meant she was now living with a guy too, although I doubted he could pay her enough to do his laundry.

"So, did you bring me something fancy?" I asked.

"Some of my best stuff," she said. "What's it for?"

I sighed. "Colin's taking me to the ballet."

"Seriously?" She whistled. "Classy."

"You see the problem."

She laughed. "What—is he trying to impress you?"

"Not exactly. His sister is in the ballet. A dancer. We're going to opening night, and then we're going to meet her and Colin's brother after."

She whistled. "He doesn't do anything half-assed, does he? Well, I brought three different options. Come on."

We crept up the creaking stairs, past Bailey's half-open door, and into the bedroom.

I immediately rejected the elegant, black, form-fitting dress, knowing it wouldn't flatter my lack of curves.

Shelly and I were the same size, but if her body type was Tinkerbell, mine was Peter Pan.

Next was a gown with a sequined silver bodice and gray, gauzy skirts. I'd been pregnant during my prom and felt no need to re-create the experience now. Pass.

The last one I had never seen before. Pink and silky with a modest neckline, the fabric gathered below the bust and then flared out into asymmetrical curves ending below my knees, almost like petals.

"Oh," I said, awestruck.

"You like it?" Shelly asked.

"I do, but—" I glanced at her, a bit surprised. It was so bright, so flirty, and she hated to be the cliché of her profession.

She looked pleased. "It's for you."

I opened my mouth, but she cut my protests short. "No complaining. And no calculating how many bags of diapers this dress could pay for. You don't need to worry about that anymore, remember?"

"Well, she still needs to poop," I muttered, but it did nothing to mask my delight. How long had it been since I'd had new clothes? Plastic flip-flops from Target didn't quite count.

I put it on—perfection. It was pretty and feminine and everything I'd always wanted to be but wasn't. Of course Shelly had known. I wanted to hug her, but she wasn't really a fan of touching.

"Thank you." I gave my skirts a flick, enjoying the way they swished against my bare legs. "You're like my fairy godmother. Now I can go to the ball."

"But you already bagged the prince," she said lightly.

Dismayed, I said, "You *are* mad."

"I'm not." She put her hand on my forearm and looked me in the eyes. "I'm not."

A slam of the door alerted us to Colin's arrival. By the time steady footsteps trekked up the stairs and to the doorway, I'd already fled to the bathroom.

"Just a minute," I called out. I wanted to brush away my pizza breath and freshen up my makeup before Colin saw me. Tonight had to be perfect.

Through the door, I heard the murmurs of Shelly and Colin, and I stepped up the pace. They'd gotten along well so far, but no need to press my luck.

When I opened the bathroom door, Shelly and the other dresses had vanished. She was probably already curled up in the armchair in Bailey's room with a book.

Colin stood at the window, looking out at the street. He still wore his jeans and T-shirt from work at the restaurant. His suit was laid out on the bed where I'd left it.

He turned, saw me, and froze. Framed by the soft evening glow, I couldn't see his face. I swayed, swishing softly. "Do you like it?" I asked.

A slight nod.

That left something to be desired.

"Are you sure?" What if he really didn't like the dress? What if it wasn't the right thing to wear to the ballet? What if he was tired of me? For all I knew, I was just the flavor of the week. Intuition was nice, but it wasn't security.

Sometimes his terseness could be downright unnerving. I didn't want to mess this up, but at this point how would I even know until he kicked my ass to the curb?

I took a deep breath and approached him, all timidity. "Are you sure this is okay?" I asked.

He nodded.

"Tell me the truth," I said.

"It's a nice dress." His leashed body and hot eyes said he liked it very much.

I blinked up at him. "Really?"

"Yes."

A smile spread across my face. "You're sweet."

I threw my arms around him. He stiffened and then put his arms around me too. And wow, I guess it *was* okay, considering the thickness I felt press against my hip.

"Hey." I put my hand on his cock through his jeans. "I can take care of that."

His hips backed away. "After the ballet, or we're never getting out of here."

"Are you sure?" I mused. "You don't want me to kneel down right here in front of you, with my new dress on, and make you feel better?"

I would've sworn I had him, but he tightened—all over—and then shook his head on a long exhale. "Later," he said.

Then he went into the bathroom to put on his suit.

He looked just like I knew he would. Perfect.

✧ ✧ ✧

WE DROVE TO the theater in silence. I rehearsed sophisticated-sounding things to say to his brother and sister. When we arrived, seating hadn't begun yet, so Colin got us drinks from the bar. Turned out rich people liked to get drunk too. Same beer, triple the price. None of the cocktail tables had any chairs, so we found an empty one to stand around. As soon as we'd settled, Colin got a call on his cell. He stepped off to the side, just out of earshot, but not so far that I couldn't hear his voice rise. I still couldn't make out his words, but I felt his anger. One word slipped through a few times: "No."

Colin returned to the table, frustration seeping through his stoic mask.

"Who was that?" I asked.

"My brother."

I tensed. He and his hold on Colin were still a sore subject for me, but I knew I had to make nice. "He's on his way?"

Colin shook his head. "He doesn't like crowds. We'll stop by his house after."

We drank. My mind scrambled desperately for a topic but came up empty. The solemnity was unnatural for me, and the more desperate I became for a topic, the more inappropriate the suggestions in my mind became. Finally the tension got to be too much, and I burst out, "I've never been to a ballet before. It's weird walking on carpet in high heels."

He said nothing.

"You've been before...right?" I asked.

"Just to see Rose." His sister.

"I'm worried I'll do something stupid."

"You won't," he said.

I bit my lip. "We got a book about the ballet from the library. I promised to tell Bailey all about the real thing later."

We fell into silence, with my lame words echoing in my head.

Then Colin said, "One day we'll bring her with us."

I curled against his side in answer, my chest feeling too full. The awkwardness fell away, and everything was perfect again.

CHAPTER SEVENTEEN

I HADN'T REALIZED exactly how long ballets were. Angelina the ballet-dancing rat from Bailey's books left something to be desired in her descriptions. Okay, so I hadn't really known what to expect, but too many people dancing in repetitive swirls for two and a half hours wasn't it. Colin's brother had the right idea after all. Crowds, my ass.

After the curtains closed, we waited backstage.

"Your sister looked really great," I said.

Colin nodded. He'd pointed her out to me, though I had no idea how he'd been able to tell her apart.

A beautiful woman with stark black hair, dark eyes, and a stunning smile emerged from the crowd.

Colin gave her a brief hug. "You were great."

So this was Rose. She looked glamorous, almost ethereal, and I felt incredibly awkward. "That was beautiful," I said. "You looked great."

Rose smiled at me with open curiosity and appraisal in her eyes. "Thank you. Colin told me about you. I'm glad to finally meet you."

"Thanks. You too." Though that wasn't entirely true. Colin hadn't told me much of anything about her. I only hoped she didn't ask for specifics.

"You have a...baby, don't you?"

"Yes." I couldn't get a read on the undercurrent, whether it was the standard weirdness about my obvious age or whether she didn't want her brother dating someone with a child. "A girl. She's twenty months."

"Where's her father?" Rose asked. I knew she didn't mean where he was physically. She meant, where was he while me and my child were freeloading off her brother.

"Rose," Colin warned.

I put my hand on his arm. "It's a fair question, but it's kind of a long story." A long story, starting with "No" and ending with a plus sign on a stick.

"I see." Rose glanced at Colin's glowering face—not that she looked particularly cowed—before shrugging. "Just looking out for my little brother."

I blinked, then looked over and up at her little brother, all five feet ten inches and one hundred and eighty pounds of him.

"Stop," he said. I could feel his tension under my hand.

Crap, starting a fight between them was the last thing I needed to do tonight. I didn't need him to take offense for me, not for this. "It's okay," I said to Colin.

He glanced down at me and then, with a deep breath, visibly relaxed.

Rose's eyebrows rose as she watched our interactions. "You know," she said. "I just might end up liking you after all."

It was hardly the ringing endorsement I'd hoped for at the beginning of the night. But then again, it was better than how things could have gone, considering how she'd been gunning for me at the start.

Once we made our good-byes, I was ready to drag Colin out of there. But he was even more eager than I, his long strides pulling ahead of my hurried steps. Once we were back in the comfort of his truck, I sank into the faded fabric of the seats, soft in a way that can only come from wear, and breathed a sigh of relief.

COLIN'S BROTHER, PHILIP, lived in a mansion.

I wasn't sure what I'd been expecting. With Colin's modest home, casual clothes, and rough build, maybe a tight-knit little family. I gaped at the sprawling building, probably in some sort of architectural style that had a name, like deco or postmodern or something, and started to doubt the tight-knit family scenario.

It dawned on me how incredibly, impossibly Colin was beyond my reach. His house was beautiful but normal. But his family. Shit. His sister in the ballet. His brother with a mansion and a lawyer on tap.

What the hell was I doing here?

Oh, right. Saving my ass. From Andrew. Like a total user.

No wonder Rose had been suspicious of me. I was everything she feared.

Despite the chilly night air, warmth invaded my

hands, and I glanced down to see Colin's large hands rubbing mine between his own. I looked up at him. "I don't…"

He cocked his head. "What's wrong?"

"I just… It's so big."

"Yeah." He shrugged. "It's mostly for show. Don't worry."

He squeezed my hands. I wished I could believe him. I trusted Colin. But he hadn't seen how his brother was using him. And Colin hadn't expected his sister to confront me. It seemed to me that he had a blind spot where his family was concerned.

But we needed Philip for the lawyer, and besides, I had hopes that I could get in his family's good graces. It was clearly important to Colin. I would do this for him.

I squeezed his hands back, and we walked up the steps.

We were let in by a man who seemed to know Colin but who didn't look or speak to me directly. I looked to Colin for an introduction, but he seemed not to notice.

Surely Colin would know the way. It was clear he'd been there many times. But the man led us to an empty room and then left. A butler, of sorts.

The room screamed masculinity, a portrait of brown tones lined in black. I squinted at the framed sepia photograph nearest me—a matador and a bull. Very subtle.

"Colin. Are you sure…?" I didn't even know how to end the sentence. This felt all wrong.

"Trust me," he said.

I couldn't tell him no. Over the warning bells clanging in my head and through the tense knot in my stomach, I trusted Colin. So I sat down in one of the chairs, the plush leather welcoming my body like a bed of quicksand.

Colin sat in the chair next to me, also sinking low.

Neither of us spoke, but I was determined not to second-guess him again tonight. He didn't deserve that from me.

The click of shoes on wood announced the arrival of a tall man, leaner than Colin, and darker. He was dressed in a white dress shirt and black slacks, but he wore them as effortlessly as sweats. And when he stepped forward into the lamplight, I saw that his face was disfigured on one side, but it was hard to say what exactly was wrong with it. At least without staring, which I tried hard not to do.

I must have failed, though, because the sharpness in his voice held a reprimand. "You must be Allison Winters."

"Allie," I offered, shrinking into the chair even as I told my feet to stand. Colin was made of sterner stuff and stood.

"Philip," Colin greeted.

Philip swung his gaze to Colin and raised his eyebrows. "You've been absent." Every word was clipped, like it was cut off a second too soon.

"You know why." Colin spoke evenly. "Where's

Laramie?"

"Late, as usual. I'd love to fire him for it if he wasn't so fucking useful." Philip grimaced and threw a nod in my direction. "Pardon my language."

Ha! That was a trip. If he thought I was a lady enough to watch his speech, then maybe there was hope for me yet. But this was stupid. I'd been silent this entire time.

"Nice to meet you." It came out as a croak. Neither man acknowledged me.

"Any news?" Colin asked, his demeanor excluding me.

"A few packages arrived last week," Philip replied, "but we're seeing delays all over the place. I'll need you to look into it."

Colin nodded as if he'd expected as much.

"Bad enough the quality issues," Philip said. "Now with shipping trouble too. It's gotta be a setup."

"I'll take care of it," Colin said.

Philip inclined his head as if that settled things. I wondered if I could have as much trust in Colin as that.

I let my mind drift while they talked shop. I'd gone to the parenting clinic for testing and contraception earlier today. The doctor had been different, but the nurse had been the same as two years ago. She hadn't recognized me. I'd gritted my teeth against their vacant expressions and impersonal touches in my most private areas, but at least that was better than the alternative.

Laramie joined us soon after. Laramie the Lawyer,

though I kept that moniker to myself. He had soft features and kind eyes, all the better to trust him with. He, at least, was introduced formally to me. This was Drew Laramie, attorney-at-law and family friend. I was Allie Winters, the one with "the problem."

I had a short speech prepared. What I'd told Colin but with details. When Bailey was born, what her birth certificate read, how I'd supported her all this time. These things had seemed important in the light of day when I'd anticipated and dreaded this meeting.

But here, in the dark, with the men settling in and throwing their words above my head, my planned words seemed superfluous, as if the details hardly mattered. Laramie sat across from Colin. Philip served us all drinks, somehow managing to not look the least bit subservient. He served me first, as the lady, I supposed. I brooded into my glass of water while the men were given an amber liquid.

"It looks like he hasn't filed yet, but that doesn't mean anything," Laramie said, finally addressing the case. "These things take time."

"And you know we'd rather avoid that altogether," said Philip.

"I understand. I have Roark looking into his background. If we can find something appropriate..." Laramie let the sentence die as he took a sip from the drink Philip handed him.

"That's risky," Colin said.

Laramie nodded. "Hard to say how a man'll react

until he's pressed into a corner. You mentioned paying him off, but that carries its own risks. Technically there'd be no guarantee he wouldn't file at some future date or press for more money."

"Oh, he'll stick to the deal," Philip said.

Laramie smiled without humor. "There's persuasion, but you don't need me for that."

God, no more violence. *Please.*

"She doesn't want that," Colin said.

They paused in unison and looked at me.

"Definitely not," I said. Which seemed to work, because they resumed talking around me, about negotiations and agreements. Riddles cloaked in ordinary words. At least there was no more talk of persuasion.

It was like I'd stumbled into some sort of Mad Hatter's tea party. I should speak up, I knew. I should advocate for Bailey, but despite the questionable ethics of some of their suggestions, they seemed to have a much better grasp on the possible solutions than I did.

If only Philip would look at me when he talked about me.

Laramie did, giving the occasional sympathetic glance, particularly when he mentioned Bailey specifically. Colin also looked at me with his usual impassivity, though he directed his comments at the other men.

Philip looked at the other men and, on occasion, at the air beside me. Never at me. After Andrew, I'd lost any claim to be a great judge of character, but everything about Philip made me nervous.

I trusted Colin, and he trusted Philip. Colin seemed to think that was enough, but I was starting to realize trust didn't work by proxy.

Laramie's eyes caught mine, an apology in them. "This man, did he ever hurt you?"

"What?" The very worst liar in the world, my eyes widened and my hands clenched.

"If he did," Laramie said carefully, "it would certainly help our case. Give us leverage."

I stared into his gentle eyes with my mouth open.

"Allie?" Colin said, but I couldn't look at him.

Laramie was silent, watching me.

I'd thought about confessing all to Colin, but it wouldn't be like this. I couldn't possibly bare all my sins, all my shame in this room full of strangers. A room full of men. I was already the gold digger, the slut, the problem. I wouldn't also be the victim.

Besides, violence had already been discussed once tonight. I didn't want Andrew hurt, though I wouldn't let myself think too hard on that. And I certainly didn't want Colin picking a fight, possibly injuring himself, possibly in trouble with the law. Hurting himself in the process because he thought he needed to fight to keep the people he cared about near him.

"No," I said.

And then stronger, turning to look at Colin. "No. He didn't hurt me."

The lie was a small stab to my stomach, which was good. I deserved no less for deceiving Colin, even if it was for his own good. Or maybe it wasn't a lie, if I thought of all my date nights. Asking for sex, for pain, in a sick bid for control, but that was an illusion. I'd never had control, and this farce of a consultation only underscored it. Those men hadn't hurt me, Andrew hadn't hurt me, not nearly so much as I'd hurt myself.

CHAPTER EIGHTEEN

COLIN'S HOUSE WAS quiet. After I shut the door behind a groggy Shelly, Colin reached back behind my neck and pulled me in for a kiss. He backed me up right there, the cool wall against my shoulders a contrast from his hot hands gripping my hips and his tongue invading my mouth.

My mind reeled from the earlier conversation. Like the flashing pictures in a slot machine, my emotions ran from guilt to fear to anger. And then frustration with myself. I was getting what I wanted; I should be happy. He pressed his mouth down the side of my neck. Should be happy.

"God," he muttered. "This dress."

Pride sparked in me, a welcomed respite. His arousal was thick, insistent. I struggled to catch up as we all but mated in the hallway, minus the intercourse.

Colin's hand parted my legs and stroked me.

I shut my eyes tight as if I could lock out my thoughts and just feel. His fingers were thick at my entrance, the calluses providing a delicious friction. His body loomed large around me, shielding me from the outside world. His lips on mine were hot and hungry.

I slickened below, just a bit. Thank God. I could do this.

I wasn't quite ready. Not physically. I was barely wet; nothing close to what Colin could bring me to, drenched and supple. Not mentally. My mind was still running replays from earlier. I wasn't in the mood right now, and my body had only begun to recognize what Colin wanted.

Colin shook with his arousal. He intimidated me with it, looking angry and intense, though I knew by now that was eagerness. I tugged him up the stairs, past the room where Bailey slept, and into his bedroom—our bedroom—and shut the door. I slipped off my panties and kicked them aside, then bent over the bed and looked back. He understood. With quick, jerky movements, he lifted my skirt and entered me.

I gasped as his cock stretched me. He paused. I wanted to do this for him. I needed to. I tilted my hips back to allow him deeper access, accepting the sharp pain without further sound.

He pulled out, almost completely, and then rammed back in. My teeth gritted together and my fingers whitened on the bedspread, but I would take it. He grabbed my shoulders and set up a rhythm of deep, punishing thrusts. He seemed lost in his pleasure, unable to notice my confusion, which I was grateful for. The air was too thick to breathe. My thoughts too murky to pierce. I didn't think I could talk—or orgasm, for that matter—if he had wanted something more than my compliance.

Colin flipped me over. I spread my legs wide, and he entered me again with deep, rooting thrusts. He slammed into me, pushing me up the bed. His wrists were beside my shoulders, and I reached up to grasp them, to anchor myself.

The pillow smashed between my head and the headboard. It was just a pillow. A soft pressure, especially considering the force of Colin's thrusts. But it triggered something in me, something hard.

Cold washed over my body. My skin prickled into goose bumps. My nipples were oversensitive, abraded against his chest. My cunt felt sore, like pulverized meat. My clit felt smashed under the thrusts of his pubic bone.

I made no move to stop the sex. This was just a way for my body to service his. My discomfort was small and well earned.

He noticed, though, and reached down to touch my clit. I jumped. "No. Don't," slipped out.

His hand stilled, and he slowed his hips to a gentle rocking. "What's wrong?"

"Just keep going."

He narrowed his eyes. "Something's wrong."

"Don't worry about it. Just…just finish."

Damned if the man wasn't as contrary as I was. He froze, still inside.

"Tell me," he demanded.

"It's nothing." As if we could have an actual conversation while his stiff cock was still lodged deep inside me.

"Just do it." I put a challenge in my voice and my eyes. "Fuck me."

I knew he wanted to by the way his hips rocked forward as if testing the waters. Coming up dry, he pulled out and sprawled across the bed, catching his breath.

I felt hot and cold at the same time. And raw. As if the physical barricades had been burned away, leaving me exposed. Helpless. All I could think about was ending this night so we could get back to normal—at least our version of normalcy.

The room was silent except for our breathing, and I had the inappropriate urge to giggle. I managed to restrain myself. All I needed was another bout of hysteria for him to peg me as crazy, not that he'd be wrong.

Colin broke the silence. "Was I too rough?"

"No." And before he could ask anything else, "I don't want to talk about it."

For the second time in our relationship, I retreated to the bathroom after sex. I slammed the door to let him know he wasn't invited this time. To ask him to follow me again.

From on top of the toilet seat, I watched the doorknob. My ears listened for footsteps or the turn of the knob, but none came. I wanted for him to come, but he never did.

I should be grateful that he'd listened to me. After feeling invisible at Philip's, after raging for control over my body for years, the fact that he'd granted my request should be bliss.

For the first time since I'd met him, I felt truly alone.

THANK YOU!

Thank you for reading! I hope you loved meeting Allie and Colin. The next book in the Chicago Underground series is HARD. Find out what secret Colin has been keeping from Allie…

And if you enjoyed ROUGH, you'll love the sexy, emotional Trust Fund duet. Both SURVIVAL OF THE RICHEST and THE EVOLUTION OF MAN are available at Amazon, iBooks, and wherever books are sold.

"Wickedly brilliant, dark and addictive!"

– Jodi Ellen Malpas,
#1 New York Times bestselling author

The price of survival… Don't miss the USA Today bestselling Endgame trilogy, starting with the critically acclaimed THE PAWN! Gabriel Miller swept into my life like a storm.

I appreciate your help in spreading the word, including telling a friend. Reviews help readers find books! Please leave a review on your favorite book site.

You can also join my Facebook group, Skye Warren's Dark Room, for exclusive giveaways and sneak peeks of future books.

SIGN UP FOR SKYE WARREN'S NEWSLETTER:
www.skyewarren.com/newsletter

Turn the page for a short excerpt from Hard…

Excerpt from HARD

"DO YOU WANT pancakes?" I asked Colin, imploring him with my eyes. *Let's be normal. Just pretend.*

His eyes narrowed, but he nodded.

Thank you.

I couldn't talk about what had happened last night, not when it was so fresh. More than that, I wasn't even sure what had happened.

I'd gone cold during sex before. In fact, I'd been cold during every sexual encounter I'd ever had, except with Colin. Never with Colin, until last night.

I piled three pancakes, the top one fresh off the skillet, onto a plate and carried it into the dining room. Colin sat, not at the head of the table, but near the foot, next to Bailey. Right in the syrup splash zone.

"Waka!" said Bailey. She was coated in syrup and pancake crumbs, from the tips of her sticky hair to her grubby, outstretched fingers.

"Good morning," Colin replied to her, with the same gravity with which he'd accepted my offer of pancakes and peace. Satisfied, Bailey returned to sculpting her soggy pile of pancake. I set the plate down in front of Colin.

"Coffee?" I offered.

"Please," he answered.

I returned to the kitchen, which I already knew like my own, and brewed the coffee. More baby talk trilled from the dining room, but I figured I'd best let them get on without me. I would try my hardest to keep Bailey in line, but if Colin was truly averse to the mess or the noise of a child, then this wasn't going to work.

A string of warbled sounds. Low tones. The bang of tiny fists on the high chair tray punctuated with a shriek.

I rushed into the dining room, prepared for the worst. Bailey fussing or throwing a tantrum. Colin angry and splashed with syrup.

What I found was Colin sliding a handful of pancake squares onto Bailey's tray. A slice of the pancakes from his plate was missing, now replaced with Bailey's pancake lump.

He turned to look at me, all seriousness. "She wanted to trade."

Books by Skye Warren

Endgame trilogy & Masterpiece Duet

The Pawn

The Knight

The Castle

The King

The Queen

Trust Fund Duet

Survival of the Richest

The Evolution of Man

Stripped series

Tough Love

Love the Way You Lie

Better When It Hurts

Even Better

Pretty When You Cry

Caught for Christmas

Hold You Against Me

To the Ends of the Earth

Criminals and Captives standalones

Prisoner

Hostage

Standalone Dangerous Romance

Wanderlust

On the Way Home

Beauty and the Beast

Anti Hero

Escort

For a complete listing of Skye Warren books, visit www.skyewarren.com/books

ABOUT THE AUTHOR

Skye Warren is the New York Times bestselling author of dangerous romance such as the Endgame trilogy. Her books have been featured in Jezebel, Buzzfeed, USA Today Happily Ever After, Glamour, and Elle Magazine. She makes her home in Texas with her loving family, sweet dogs, and evil cat.

Sign up for Skye's newsletter:
www.skyewarren.com/newsletter

Like Skye Warren on Facebook:
facebook.com/skyewarren

Join Skye Warren's Dark Room reader group:
skyewarren.com/darkroom

Follow Skye Warren on Instagram:
instagram.com/skyewarrenbooks

Visit Skye's website for her current booklist:
www.skyewarren.com

COPYRIGHT

Print Edition

Cover design by Book Beautiful
Cover photograph by Sara Eirew
Formatting by BB eBooks

Made in the USA
Las Vegas, NV
06 May 2024